OF SAND AND STONE

A Time Travel Romance

LAUREN SMITH

To all my historical romance readers who made me brave enough to dip my fingertips into time travel.

Rebecca Clark could stare at naked chiseled men all day, which was a good thing considering it was her job. Well, a part of it. As the curator of a small New England art museum, she looked at naked men all the time.

But they weren't real men. They were marble, not flesh and blood. For the last three years she'd specialized in marble sculpture collections, and right now she was staring at the perfect specimen.

It was carved from a single slab of exquisite Italian marble by some obscure sculptor in London more than two hundred years ago. The only clues as to the sculptor's identity were two words carved into the statue's base: "Oath" and "Pride." The Adonis—it had to be Adonis, as perfect as he was—stood proudly at six feet tall, though the statue was actually seven, given its foot-high pedestal.

As the lights of the room illuminated the statue's broad shoulders and smooth abs, she let herself wonder how long he had been hidden away in the large packing crate he'd arrived in, now lying discarded behind him, straw from the wooden crate littering the floor.

"Well, he looks ready to me," a man in gray coveralls announced as he brushed straw off his hands. He and his partner had spent the last hour carefully moving the statue through the warehouse and into the temporary exhibit that had come from London.

"Thank you, Stan. See you tomorrow." Although Rebecca planned to stay another couple of hours to finish the paperwork on the exhibits, she didn't want her staff to work late. She genuinely liked working with everyone at the museum, except for her boss.

"Thanks, Ms. Clark. Have a good night." The pair picked up the crate and carried it out of the exhibit room, leaving a trail of packing material behind them. Rebecca smiled and shook her head. It could be cleaned up tomorrow.

She checked her watch and sighed when she realized it was almost ten. This wasn't unusual. She was used to burning the midnight oil, and this was an exciting new exhibition. Besides, it wasn't as if she had a social life or anything—anyone—to go home to. A flicker of embarrassment made her cheeks flame.

I shouldn't be ashamed of working hard and still being single.

But no matter how much she told herself that it didn't seem to change how she felt. It seemed like the world judged a woman's value by whether she could catch and marry a decent man. Rebecca wanted to be in a relationship, not because society expected it of her, but because she wanted to be loved. But after all the men she'd dated in the last several years she'd given up on finding a good one.

Her gaze was drawn to the marble man and his lean, exquisite body with slightly sloped muscles and bulging cords of sinew. Everything was carved so perfectly into the stone that she almost thought she could see them move in the right light.

He was bigger too—*down there*—than other male statues she'd seen, and far more masculine with his broad shoulders and slim hips. She couldn't help but walk a full circle around the statue to admire him... er...*it* from every angle.

Full sensual mouth, soft bedroom eyes, and literally a chiseled jaw. But the hair—tousled rock-hard waves—that was the hair of a man who'd stumbled from the bed of his lover before posing for the artist. He was gorgeous.

Real men didn't look like this. Men were petty

and selfish. They clung to women, used them or cheated on them, especially the good-looking guys.

She shook her head, banishing the dark thoughts. It wasn't true. There were good men in the world— fathers, brothers, husbands, friends. But aside from her own father, she'd never encountered a good man in her life. If there was a lazy, spoiled, or rotten man out there, she'd found him and dated him. Not by choice, of course. People were clever about hiding their faults, and she always found new ways of being fooled.

The pattern was always the same. First she'd be smitten with a man, and she would date him casually. They'd enjoy each other's company, the sex would curl her toes, and she'd hope it would lead to something more. Three to six months later she'd find herself exhausted and fed up with the cooking and the cleaning up after a man only to have lackluster sex—*if* she was lucky enough to snag his attention before he passed out on the couch to the news. Even when she was lucky, she'd be so tired that all she could do was lie there and let him get his, without ever getting hers.

It meant that she was still single at thirty-two, but she'd *almost* come to accept that fate. Better to be alone than to be totally unhappy. Rebecca stared up at the beautiful statue, and with a bashful smile, she reached up to touch his hip. The marble was cool beneath her fingers, but she jumped and pulled her hand back when she felt a little electric spark. She studied the statue, trying to figure out how she could get a static zap from marble. Then she returned her hand to the stone again, laughing at her foolishness.

"Why couldn't a man like you be real?" Her soft voice echoed in the darkened gallery. "Someone tall, handsome, strong, yet caring when I need him to be, and sexy as hell."

But it was a dream and nothing more. Men like this didn't exist, couldn't exist.

A sudden chill stole through the room, and Rebecca curled her arms around her shoulders, hugging herself as she gazed at the man's stone face.

"See you tomorrow, handsome." She bit her lip, and with a shy smile at the statue, she turned and walked back to her office. There was a mountain of paperwork waiting for her, though all she wanted was to go home with a man like the one on the pedestal in the gallery.

❧

MOONBEAMS CUT THROUGH THE WIDE WINDOWS, playing with shadows in the art gallery. The figures in the paintings were silent but watchful, as if waiting for something to happen. There wasn't a sound to be heard throughout the gallery. Everything was still and silent...

A woman in a white gown appeared, as if the moonlight itself had coalesced into human form. She smiled as she made her way to the statue in the middle of the room, her eyes both playful and hard. Its white stone gleamed like solid moonlight in the darkness.

"Hello, Devon," she said as she brushed a fingertip along its marble thigh. "Are you ready to be a good boy and please your goddess?"

An electric pulse shot through the stone, and she chuckled. So the mortal still had some fight in him, even after two hundred years.

She studied the stone figure's face, and her eyes sharpened. "Hear me, Devon Blake. You were punished for failing to please your goddess and seeking only your own pleasure in my arms. It was my right and duty to punish you. Now I am feeling lenient and merciful. Do *not* make me regret such soft emotions." She studied the words "Oath" and "Pride" inscribed in the stone. She'd made an oath to herself to punish Devon for his pride. A smile twitched the corners of her lips. The words oath and pride also spelled her name: Aphrodite. A little goddess humor she couldn't resist indulging in.

She paused, brushing a hand down the diaphanous white gown that hung from her shoulders and clung to her full curves. "You must prove to a mortal woman that you are able to please her without sating your own lust for an entire week. If you cannot do this, and fail to win that woman's love because of your selfishness, then you will return to stone. And it will be far more than two hundred years before I grant you another chance."

The gallery vibrated with the goddess's words. The spell—or rather the curse—settled into the stones and the frames of the paintings and, most importantly, into the marble statue of the man once known as Devon Blake.

The goddess glanced about the room, eyeing the silent witnesses to her curse before she faced the frozen man.

"She who has woken you with her touch shall be the woman who will set you free—if you have the strength to put her desires before your own."

And with that, the goddess vanished. The gallery seemed to sigh its own quiet relief that a goddess had come and gone without leaving a path of destruction in her wake. Instead, she'd left a lingering sense of dark enchantment that could only be broken by the power of love.

Such was a fitting curse from the goddess Aphrodite.

Devon Blake, the fifth Earl of Richmond, heard every word Aphrodite had spoken. For two centuries, he had been able to hear everything and yet see nothing of what was in front of his marble eyes. He had been trapped in a nightmare, unable to speak or cry out. He had spent the last two hundred years traveling from museum to museum around the world, and he could hear Aphrodite's mocking laugh each time he reached a new city. In his frozen stone state, he'd been able to hear bits of conversations of people around him but could not see, could not truly grasp how different the world must be around him now.

How much life have I missed while trapped in stone?

He had been reduced to a creature put on display, to be marveled at and gawked at like a common street performer—and a naked one at that—as opposed to the aristocrat he'd once been, with power, good looks, and wealth.

And it was all Aphrodite's fault.

Had he not come across her in a quiet corner of Covent Garden one night while the fireworks burst over his head and whispered laughter slithered through the hedges and blooms, he might never have made the mistake of bedding her. His mind howled at the memory of that night, how he'd slaked his lust upon the goddess's beauty and had not one care for her pleasure before he'd abandoned her.

It was my downfall, to care only about myself.

He'd walked not twenty steps before he'd heard the booming shout from behind him.

"*How* dare *you walk away from me, mortal!*" And in seconds, his heart had stopped, his world had crumbled into darkness, and he'd been imprisoned in this marble nightmare where he could experience no sight or touch, but hear only what happened around him.

Now he had a chance to undo his mistake and earn Aphrodite's forgiveness. He had to last seven days with one woman and not seek his own pleasure, only hers. He could do it. He had to.

But who would be the woman to free him of this curse? He thought of the woman who'd been in the gallery a few moments before Aphrodite. He'd had no eyes to see her, yet he'd felt her hand on his cold stone skin, and his body had responded with desire at her sultry whisper, longing for a perfect man. How could her touch have made him feel something when nothing else had since he'd been transformed into stone?

There was something in her plea that had called to him, and he had cried out inside his mind for her to keep touching him. It had been too long since he'd been a living, breathing man with a body to touch and hands to touch with. Too long...

He listened to the sounds of the quiet gallery now, the distant chime of a clock, the creak of a wall settling into place, and he wondered where he was. Somewhere in America, if he had heard the movers correctly. He'd lost track of how many times he'd been moved and had long since ceased to care. It hadn't mattered—until now.

The woman's words echoed in his mind, taunting him. *"Why couldn't a man like you be real?"*

And then it happened. His skin began to burn, and his insides churned as though he was going to be sick. Though he couldn't see or move, his head was spinning and he wished he could stand the dizzying feeling that...

His body hit the cold wooden floor with a thud. For a moment he feared he would shatter until he realized it had been flesh that hit the hard floor. Every muscle in him screamed in agony. After two centuries of being stone, he couldn't breathe, couldn't move.

An agonized gasp escaped his lips, the sound ricocheting off the walls of the room around him. He kept his eyes closed, panting as he lay on the floor, his body awkwardly twisted, but there was no helping it. He wasn't sure how long he lay there, listening to his heartbeat pound against his eardrums, before he heard a sound.

"Hello? Is someone there?"

It was a woman's voice. The realization crept into his mind as he focused on breathing. He might as well have had dust in his lungs, after all the time they hadn't been used.

"Hello?" the woman said again.

This time, Devon forced his eyes to open, then promptly clamped them back shut. The moonlight that swept in through the windows was too bright. He couldn't take it.

"Oh my God!" the woman said with a gasp from close by. The sound of her footfalls and then the touch of her hands—it was shocking, and he tensed, emitting a low groan of pain.

"What happened? Are you okay?" The woman's speech was hurried and her accent definitely American. Warm feminine hands touched his shoulder, his lower back, his arm, and then his cheek.

"Please don't be dead," she whispered. "Oh God, please don't be dead."

"Not. Dead. Need. A. Moment." Every word he muttered had to be dragged painfully out of his unused throat.

"Thank God!"

Her exclamation made him chuckle. It was not the Christian God she should be thanking but a very clever goddess. He'd spent the last two centuries trying to come to grips with the theological implications of that fact, and he was no closer to an answer now than the day he'd been turned to stone.

"What are you doing in here? How did you get in?" the woman asked as she helped him to sit up. He could feel her trembling as she touched him. The ladies of his era would have screamed and likely fainted at the sight of a strange unclothed man appearing out of nowhere.

"I swear I mean you no harm, my lady..." His throat felt like shards of glass had cut him deep. "I'm afraid I had an...unfortunate accident."

"I think I should call the police. I'm sure they can help you...er..." The woman stumbled over her words.

Devon wasn't sure if *police* were the men of law and order from his century, but he could guess by her tone that they would likely take him away, which would damn him forever.

"Please, no, I beg you. Do not summon

the...*police*. I can explain why I am here if you but give me a moment to rest." He rubbed at his eyes, and then, blinking owlishly, he opened them. It took him a moment before he could bear the bright moonlight, and then he got a better look at the woman.

She sat on the floor beside him, in a knee-length tweed skirt that flared out. She wore a waistcoat of the same tweed, with a white blouse beneath and strange leather shoes with heels. It was quite a fetching and certainly scandalous-looking outfit that immediately caught his attention.

Devon looked to the woman's face, startled by the warm brown eyes and the little upturned nose that was smattered with light freckles. A pair of rimless spectacles perched on her nose, giving her a scholarly look. Her hair was pulled back in a chignon with a...a pencil sticking out of the back? Did the woman know she had a writing utensil stuck in her hair? Surely she didn't. Only artists and craftsmen used pencils. What did that make this woman?

"You're naked!" The woman's gaze dropped to his lap, and he cursed as he glanced down. His body was already showing signs of interest in the woman, and he was not about to forget Aphrodite's words of warning regarding his own lust.

"That I am, my lady. Could you please tell me what year it is and where exactly I am?" He sighed and rubbed at his face, relieved that he didn't have to shave, at least not yet. That was one thing he hadn't missed in all those years trapped in stone. "And perhaps something to cover myself with?"

"What *year*? If you're going to tell me to come with you because some robot is trying to kill me, you can forget it. I've seen the movie."

Robot? Movie?

"I'm sorry, I'm not sure I understand you. Please, where am I?"

"You're in Mistlethwaite, near Boston. Oh God..." The woman choked suddenly, and her distress made his heart race. "You shipped yourself here in a freight container, didn't you? I heard about some magician doing that stunt once. But why did you do it naked?"

He looked around the exhibit and saw a banner announcing the current exhibition: "Meeting the Masters—Classical Art Exhibit 2018"

So it was true. That night he'd been in the gardens with Aphrodite had been in the year 1816. His mind reeled. He'd known it had been two hundred years, yet seeing the evidence of it now put a knot in his stomach.

"Two hundred bloody years... You damned bitch!"

He heard a soft, lilting chuckle drift down from the rafters of the room. Aphrodite was always watching.

"You're starting to scare me," the woman whispered, backing away, and then she looked around the room. "Wait. Where is the statue? It was just here..." Her head lowered as she stared at his feet and the faint sheen of dust that surrounded him on the stone floor, mixed with the scattered packing material.

"I'm sorry," Devon muttered, wondering how he was going to explain that he *was* the statue. "I should not speak thus in front of a lady. Please accept my apologies." He looked her way again, focusing on her face, the soft brown eyes, the pale creamy skin that was full of a rosy blush, and smooth petal-soft-looking lips. Damn, she would be a delight to please in bed.

"Okay. I'm not going to lie—I'm still freaking out. Seriously, how the hell did you get into the gallery, and why are you naked?" She gave him a respectable, safe distance. "Sane, rational people don't go running around naked. Only crazy serial killers do, and I swear, if you try anything..."

"What is a serial killer?" he asked. He was not a killer of any kind, except during the occasional hunt for foxes, deer, or pheasants.

"You expect me to believe you don't know what a serial killer is? That's *exactly* what a serial killer would say." Rebecca took another step back, and each time she did, it terrified him. She was the only thing keeping him from returning to stone, and he could not let her leave him.

Devon raised his hands in a placating gesture.

"I'm afraid you would not believe me if I told you the truth of how I came here and why."

She narrowed her eyes. "Why don't you try me? As long as you don't claim to be from the future on a mission to save mankind or something insane like that..."

A rough chuckle escaped him. This would prove to be interesting. "Nay, I'm not from the future, but the past. Two hundred years ago, I had the misfortune of bedding the goddess Aphrodite. She cursed me for being a selfish bastard. She trapped me in the marble stone you were admiring a short while before." He waved at the empty pedestal behind him.

The woman's eyes went from him to the empty pedestal. "But...that's not possible. You can't be..."

"I'm afraid I am." His tone turned gruff as he tried to stand, but his legs wobbled and he fell back down like a newborn foal.

The woman stared at him and then the pedestal for a long moment. "Okay, so let's pretend I believe you, just a little. Gods and goddesses aren't exactly known for their forgiving nature. Hell, I remember reading once that a woman was turned into a spider just for claiming she was good at weaving. Cursed people tend to stay cursed. So why did Aphrodite change her mind now?"

Devon smiled crookedly. This lass was a smart one, and he liked that. It wasn't often in the past that he'd enjoyed the company of intelligent women. He'd only ever been focused on what was underneath their skirts, but this woman was rather refreshing. Perhaps the goddess had done him a favor when she'd chosen this woman for him.

"I believe she thought you would be well suited to the challenge of my redemption."

"Redemption?"

"It seems Aphrodite believes you are in need of an exceptional and unselfish lover. She thought I would be the answer to your amorous woes."

Rebecca tilted her head to one side. "The answer? What does that mean?"

"It means that the curse requires me to pleasure you for an entire week without receiving any of my own."

"Excuse me?" Her voice rose sharply in pitch. "You're not touching me, mister. I don't want you to—"

"Do not fret. I'll not touch you unless you wish it." He made another attempt to stand, and when he started to stumble she caught his arm and steadied him.

"Look, mister, I think I should take you to the hospital."

"No!" he barked out. When she pulled away, he ducked his head. "I'm sorry. I cannot go there. I just need to rest, eat a bit, and sleep." He was suddenly weary, as though he hadn't slept in, well, two hundred years. While he'd been trapped in stone, he hadn't been able to sleep. Ever.

"But..." The woman hesitated. He offered her his most hopeful, non-seductive smile. And like hundreds of women before her, she caved. She looked back to the empty pedestal, as if confirming the statue's disappearance one more time before agreeing to help. "Look, I can take you to my place, but you're sleeping on the couch, and I swear to God if you try anything—and I mean *anything*—I'll have the cops on your ass before you breathe. Understood?"

He nodded. He had no idea what cops were or why he wouldn't want them on his ass, but it sounded rather unpleasant.

"Follow me." She started to walk away, and he followed her, his legs still a little shaky, but the more he walked, the better he felt. The stiffness was coming out of his joints, and his lungs didn't burn as much. Soon he would be at this woman's home, in her bed, and with luck, fulfilling his promise to Aphrodite so he could secure his freedom.

Just seven days without my own release—I can do that, can't I?

3

This is insane. I'm insane.

Rebecca tried not to look at the man who sat in the passenger seat of her small Volvo. He was naked as the day he was born, except for her spare coat, which she'd had him wrap around his waist before they'd gotten to the car. He seemed unashamed of his nudity, and every time he caught her looking, he just laughed.

And it was such a nice laugh too. Rich, dark, full of erotic promises. The men she'd dated didn't laugh like that, like they were thinking about how you would taste and then chuckling when you squirmed as they licked you until you screamed their name. Those were just the men in her fantasies. And yet he acted as if he was going to...

She needed to distract herself fast.

"What's your name?"

"Apologies. My unusual situation is no excuse for poor manners. I am Devon Blake, at your service. And you are?" His rich accent was music to her ears. Of course he had a name like Devon Blake. A sexy, elegant, masculine name.

She focused on the road as she drove them to her small house, which was only a few blocks from the museum. "I'm Rebecca Clark."

"It's a pleasure to meet you, Miss Clark."

"Please, call me Rebecca." Her response made him smile wide and wickedly. Her heart fluttered. She shouldn't be reacting to a stranger like this. He could be crazy, likely *was* crazy. He might even be a serial killer—a very hot one with a killer smile.

Focus!

"So you won't tell me how you really ended up naked in a gallery or where the marble statue went. Fine. Is there someone I should call to come and get you and take you...home?" She'd have to figure out what happened to the statue soon, otherwise her boss would fire her in an instant, but she had to figure out what to do with Devon first.

"Call?" he asked, his dark brows rising. "How do you mean?"

"On the phone. You have to know what that is, right?" She reached a stoplight and took a second to pull her cell phone out of her purse. He took it from her, staring at the black screen.

"Is this another one of your tricks, like this carriage that needs no horses?"

She almost laughed. He'd been startled when she'd led him to the Volvo a short time ago, and she'd had to coax him inside. She'd had to lock the doors after she'd started the engine; otherwise, he would have leapt out of the moving vehicle. It was like he'd never seen a car before.

"Curious piece of rock, like polished obsidian."

"Just press the home button." She gestured to the small indent of a button.

His elegant fingers touched upon the home screen button, and he pursed his lips, then pressed it. The screen lit up, showing a picture of her male Wheaten Terrier, Evan.

Devon dropped the phone to the floor and recoiled as though it were poisonous. "God's blood! What the bloody hell is that?"

"Calm down!" Rebecca shouted, smacking his arm as he tried to make the sign of the cross. "It's just a phone."

Devon crossed his arms over his chest and glared at the phone sourly. "Damned infernal device, that's what it is."

"Oh boy," Rebecca muttered. It was obvious

Devon needed serious help. He was completely out of touch with reality.

By the time she reached her neighborhood, he was staring at the houses along the street with awe.

"So much has changed," he whispered to himself. His voice was colored with a grief and longing she didn't understand.

"Um, right. We're at my house now, so why don't you come with me, okay? And keep the coat wrapped around your...just keep it wrapped. In case my neighbors see you." It was dark and close to one in the morning, but still, Mrs. Lesley next door was a prying old woman who loved to stick her long nose between the blinds and peer at Rebecca's house. If she saw a naked man wandering the streets, it might give the woman a heart attack.

Rebecca rushed to her front door and opened it, then gestured for Devon to hurry inside. He gripped her black coat around his waist, but it couldn't totally cover his ass. His very fine, tight-as-hell ass...

"This is a lovely home," Devon announced. He stood in the entryway and took in the butter-yellow walls of the vestibule covered in old photographs and the half-paneled walnut wood walls of the living room beyond.

"Thanks." Rebecca sighed as she leaned back against the closed door. Without warning, Evan came bounding down the stairs, streaking straight toward

Devon. He barked furiously for all of two seconds before he stood up on his hind legs, placed his front paws on Devon's bare stomach, and stretched, eagerly expecting a pat on the head.

Rebecca rolled her eyes. *So much for being a guard dog.*

Devon stroked his free hand through Evan's pale-cream fur and smiled. "I do enjoy the company of dogs. Good creatures to have about to chase rats. Sometimes better than cats."

She didn't rise to the bait and tell him that they were no longer in a century that required animals to keep houses rat free. He was just looking for an excuse to act all anachronistic on her.

"Evan, come here, you crazy dog," she cooed and knelt down to greet the only male she really trusted with her heart. He pounced on her, licking her face wildly, his soft cream-colored fur feeling like fleece beneath her hands. Yeah...Evan was the only male she'd ever really trust to love. She gazed into his bright brown eyes and tried not to laugh when his tongue lolled out of one side of his mouth. She'd spent many nights with her face buried in his fur coat, crying over her latest disappointing date. Evan was her furry soulmate. When she stopped petting him, he made a soft whining noise and pawed at her knee, reminding her she was forgetting to stroke him.

"You're spoiled, you know that? *Spoiled.*" Rebecca

laughed and then suddenly remembered Devon was standing behind her. When she straightened, and looked his way, she saw the soft way his eyes were watching her and the dog.

"You care about him," Devon said quietly.

"Yeah, he's been with me for a long time. Seven years. He's gotten me through a lot of breakups."

"Breakups?" Devon's brows rose.

"Breakups, you know, when you and the guy you're dating stop, well, dating." Geez, this guy could really play this delusional game well.

"Ahh, in my century we call that crying off. Men who do that are cowards."

"Huh, couldn't agree more on that." She muttered. "Anyway, why don't you come inside. The couch is this way." She pointed to her cozy little living room that had a soft brown leather couch and a flat-screen TV. "I'll fetch you some clothes to wear, some blankets, and a pillow."

She left Devon standing in her living room with Evan bounding around him like a puppy with a new toy. She raced upstairs and dug through her linen closet, relieved to find some old clothes from her last boyfriend stuffed in a bag she'd forgotten to take the Salvation Army. There were boxers, some shirts, and even a pair of jeans inside. It would have to do for tonight.

Devon was staring at her TV when she returned, a frown curving his sensual lips.

"Another infernal device?" he asked her, nodding at the TV. "Like your phone?"

Rebecca laughed. "You're probably the only man in the world who'd say that about a TV." She then held out the pair of boxers she'd found. "Here. You can wear these tonight."

He took the boxers and let her coat drop to the floor. She immediately looked away, trying not to stare at how huge *it* was.

"Nightclothes?" he scoffed. "I don't require them. I prefer to sleep naked." His gaze swept her from head to toe. "Feeling the sheets slide upon my skin. It is quite...liberating."

For a second Rebecca was fixated on the idea of a naked Devon in bed, luxuriating in the sensation of sleeping completely nude. She shook herself out of it. That was a dangerous train of thought she couldn't entertain. Men were trouble, and she did not need to fall for a guy like Devon who clearly had issues.

"You'll wear these because it's *my* couch, and I'm not having you sleep naked on it." She bent to retrieve her coat from the floor and left to throw it in the laundry room. It gave her a second to fan her face without being seen.

"You've stepped in it now, Rebecca," she

muttered. "Missing statue, crazy naked hot guy in your living room..."

Maybe this was a dream, some wild manifestation of her inner desires. Maybe if she went to bed in her dream and then woke up, she'd wake up for real. Yeah, that sounded like a good idea. *Put the naked, sexy, gorgeous crazy man to bed and then go to bed yourself... with sexy naked man beside you...*

She shook that tempting thought out of her head. He was clearly disturbed, and she had to get him some help first thing tomorrow morning. She could take him down to the police station and see what they thought of Mr. Man from the Past. She'd also have to report the missing statue and face the wrath of her boss.

She prayed Devon wouldn't run off in the middle of the night. He was her only chance at figuring out what had happened to the missing marble piece. If she couldn't find it, she'd end up fired—or worse, investigated as an accomplice. Her whole life would be turned upside down when the police figured out she was somehow involved in its disappearance. The thought made her stomach churn.

When she returned to the living room, Devon had donned the boxers but not the T-shirt. He was seated on the couch, running a hand along Evan's head and back in long, smooth strokes. The dog gazed at him with unrelenting hero worship.

Traitor.

"I hate to trouble you," Devon began, his voice soft and alluring, "but might I have some water? I'm afraid my throat is..." He rubbed at it. "Parched."

Rebecca rushed into the kitchen, slightly embarrassed. Ordinarily, offering a guest a drink or something to eat would have been the first thing she would have done. But then, this wasn't exactly an ordinary social situation. She peeped around the kitchen wall back into the living room. "Are you hungry?"

"I could certainly eat if you are preparing something," he said, but she could tell by the way he put a hand to his stomach that he wanted food.

"He'll have to make do with PB&J," she muttered as she whipped him up a sandwich and got him a glass of water. She didn't cook that often. There was something really depressing about cooking for one, and she didn't like keeping a ton of leftovers in the fridge.

When she placed them on the coffee table in front of him, he glanced around.

"No servants to attend you? What about your parents? Surely you don't live here alone? That's far too dangerous for a woman." He gulped down the entire glass of water and released a grateful sigh.

He was back to his time travel game again, but she decided to play along. "My parents live fifty miles away. Women in this century live on their own. We don't need to be watched over like children. And servants? I definitely don't have any. Only really, really rich people have those."

Devon chuckled as he took a bite of his sandwich. "It seems not everything has changed then. But you shouldn't live alone. I still believe it's dangerous." He took another bite and smiled. "This is quite wonderful. What is it?"

"Peanut butter and jelly." Rebecca sat down in one of her armchairs by the couch, watching him as he ate the simple sandwich as though it were a rare delicacy.

"This is good fare," he said and took another bite. "Sweet, yet nutty with just enough salt to complement it." When he was done, he set the plate on the table. He looked at the plate, and then, without a word, he stood and returned to the kitchen with it.

"What are you doing?"

"If you have no servants to attend to your needs, then I shall clean this myself, but I..." He trailed off, looking strangely bashful. Rebecca had to acknowledge that a half-naked man in her kitchen wanting to do his own dishes was...so fucking hot.

She got up and held out her hand. "Don't worry about it. I'll just—"

He held the plate away from her. "No, just show me what needs to be done." It was clear, however, that he was in awe, if not overwhelmed by the kitchen with its humming fridge and the sleek countertops and microwave.

"Just pull this handle and open the dishwasher." She showed him how to open the washer and put the dish into the rack. "I'll turn on the washer in a few minutes."

Devon stared at the washer. "It washes the dishes for you? Such magic in this century—it astounds me. He smiled a little.

Rebecca nodded. "Yeah, you'd really love the washing machine for clothes then." He didn't seem to hear her sarcasm.

"No wonder you need no servants. How extraordinary!" He was really deep into his role as a man lost in time. She had to admit it was very convincing. Which only made the matter more disconcerting.

Devon looked down at his body which was still caked with a faint layer of dust, not too much but enough that it seemed to bother him.

"Would it be too much trouble to prevail upon you for a bathing tub?" he asked.

"A bathing tub? Oh! Right," she laughed nervously. "How about a shower."

He looked toward the windows, frowning. "You bathe in the rain? But...well, I suppose if it's what people of the future do, then I will give it a go."

"No," she laughed a little, feeling definitely crazy

that she was going to have to show him a shower and explain it.

"Come with me." She lead him upstairs to her bathroom and fetched a couple of towels, setting them on the counter. She also grabbed a spare toothbrush and put it on the counter next to a tube of toothpaste.

"Okay, so this is the shower." She pulled back the shower curtain and pointed to the tub and the nozzle. "You stand beneath the shower head and you turn on the water. The letter H will give you hotter water and C will give you colder water. And be sure to pull up the lever here on bath spout or it won't work. Got it?"

He wrinkled his nose, still frowning. "I can manage," he finally said.

"Good. I'll be outside, just holler if you need me."

"Thank you." He closed the door and she listened to the sound of him undressing through the thin door. She'd seen him naked, but the thought of him standing beneath the shower, water spraying down his body made her flush with heat. The man was built like a god and it was a little hard not to fantasize about him.

The sound of the water coming out was followed by a sudden bellowing shout.

"Devon!" She opened the door and burst inside the bathroom. Devon was crouched against the back wall of the shower, sputtering as his face was being blasted by the shower head.

"Bloody cold as ice!" he gasped, shivering.

"Shit!" Rebecca hastily adjusted the temperature and reached up, angling the shower head down so it hit his chest and feet.

"You alright?" she asked, doing her best not to look down at his naked body.

He was still shivering and rubbing at his arms but he nodded. "Thank you, I was taken unawares by the temperature. It's colder that even I am used to."

"Colder?" she asked.

"Yes," he chuckled, meeting her gaze, unashamed of his nakedness. "We used to have footmen heat up buckets of water and fill copper tubs. It took ages and by the time the tub was full the water was somewhat tepid, but never frigid like this." He then scowled at the shower head.

"Well you can adjust it if you need to. Make it a little hotter or colder. I'll leave you some clothes in the hall and you can come down when you're done."

Devon nodded and she reached out, pulling the curtain closed on him and the view of his gorgeous body.

She waited a moment longer outside the bathroom, and when she was certain he was alright, she fetched a new set of boxers for him to sleep in. Then she went back downstairs and tried to watch some

TV while she waited for him. Fifteen minutes later, he came back down the stairs, his wet hair and skin damp but clean. He looked better, far better than he had all night.

"Thank you Rebecca, I very much needed that." He held out the wet towels and she ran them over the washing machine and came back to the living room. He was staring at the TV, arms crossed over his bare chest as he watched a re-run a procedural Navy drama called NCIS.

"The wonders of the age..." he murmured to himself and then turned to her.

Rebecca couldn't resist smiling. That was much more of a natural male reaction to a TV.

"Right... So, why don't you try and get some sleep on the couch, and I'll wake you in the morning, okay?"

She had no intention of telling him that she was going to take him to a doctor first thing tomorrow. That would send him running off into the night half-naked. He might get hurt. As much as she didn't need this new complication in her life right now, she hated the thought of him running away even more.

It was going to be a long night.

4

Despite how bone-weary he felt, Devon couldn't sleep. There was a strange distant humming that came from outside. He'd gotten up more than once to listen to the eerie sound and wondered what it was. Rebecca had come down the first time, worried when she'd heard the front door open. She wore a puffy robe with little pink hearts on it and stared at him bleary-eyed.

"Everything okay?" she asked, stifling a yawn with one hand.

"That sound...like a distant hive of bees. What is it?" He'd opened the door a little wider, hoping she too could hear it.

She came to join him at the doorway and peered out into the night, listening. He studied her face, struck again by her beauty, the pleasant array of her features, and the way her hair spilled around her shoulders. He gave himself a shake to stop thinking of her in that manner; otherwise, he'd have to deal with his arousal all night without relief. Aphrodite would enjoy watching him suffer, and he refused to give her the satisfaction.

"It's just the cars over on the highway," she'd finally said.

When he'd continued to stare in the distance, she'd sighed and gone back upstairs to bed. Evan had kept Devon company when he returned to the couch, his furry head resting on Devon's stomach for over an hour before he finally settled down on the floor with a heavy canine sigh.

So this was truly the future. A new millennium. A world full of frightening wonders. Like the carriage without a horse, the dishwasher that needed no servants, the lights that required no candles... He was not a man who would readily admit to fear, but he was terrified of these things that he couldn't understand. He had been a man of reason before he'd been imprisoned in stone. He'd known enough about science to think that the things he was seeing now in this home, in this world, weren't possible.

Or were they? These devices, he'd deduced, must use a form of electrical energy, and Alessandro Volta's experiments on how to store such energy were widely discussed. Yet it seemed impossible that the tiny obsidian "phone" could hold a voltaic pile within it. Could it be some type of magic?

Perhaps magic was simply a new form of science, one that mankind had unlocked while he'd been imprisoned? He would have to ask Aphrodite, if he could ever bring himself to speak to her again.

Restless, he rose from the couch and walked back into the kitchen. He looked over the tall white metal structure that hummed softly, and he approached it. It was some kind of pantry storage from what he could tell. He curled his fingers around the silver handle and tugged. It didn't budge. He saw no lock or latch keeping it shut. He pulled harder, and it came open suddenly, the contents inside the box rattling a little. Light blossomed from an unseen source, and he stared inside in fascination as a wave of cool air brushed against him.

He turned his attention to the contents of the box. Eggs, juice, milk...he could read what everything was, but he was confused by the strange packages they came in. His stomach gave another rumble, and he picked up an oddly wrapped item.

"Ball Park Bun Size Franks..." He stared at what looked like sausage meat, but he wasn't sure. He put the item back. He wasn't hungry enough to eat anything unless he was certain what it was.

There were drawers made of glass, but they

weren't heavy, nor did they feel fragile when he opened them. In fact, they didn't feel like glass at all, though he'd be hard pressed to describe what it did feel like. These drawers contained items he did recognize. Lettuce, tomatoes, onions, and other vegetables. The drawer below that contained more wrapped packages, but he could read the labels. Ham, turkey, cheese...

Devon snatched those up and carried them to the counter. A loaf of bread lay near the humming box, and he searched through the cabinets before he found a plate and a knife. Much to his surprise, however, the bread had already been sliced, and with expert precision, as was the meat and cheese. It seemed the only thing he required the knife for was spreading a bit of butter.

After a sandwich and a tall glass of milk, he stumbled back to the couch in exhaustion and curled up beneath the blankets. Evan's tail wagged, hitting the side of the couch with a rhythmic thump until the dog laid his head back down on the floor. Sleep finally claimed Devon, but he was plagued with endless dreams of mazes in gardens where he couldn't escape the sound of a goddess's laughter.

When he woke it was much later in the day, and light reflected off the surface of the object that Rebecca had called the TV, blinding him when he first opened his eyes. He was startled to find that at some point Evan had crawled onto the couch with him and was now lying across Devon's body.

The dog raised his head, panting as he watched Devon with his dark-brown eyes.

"Morning, dog." He ruffled Evan's hair, and the dog licked his hand.

"About time you woke up." Rebecca's voice made him sit up sharply, causing the dog to jump to the floor and trot over to his mistress. Devon glanced around and found her sitting at a table in the kitchen, coffee mug in hand.

Groaning, Devon sat up further. "What hour is it?"

Rebecca checked her watch. "Noon. Now that you're awake, we need to get you some clothes. Clothes that fit."

He glanced down at the tight underclothes. "Agreed. These will not do. Men of my standing never wear inexpressibles." He stood up, and she did the same.

"What are inexpressibles?" she asked.

"Scandalously tight leggings that leave little to the imagination."

"Oh," she said with a laugh, her cheeks a delightful pink shade now as she stared at him in his state of undress. "I have some clothes that will probably work to get us to the store, but my guess is they'll be tight." She went upstairs and came back down, handing him a pair of pants made of a strange blue material and a shirt of a softer fabric. She'd called them jeans and a T-shirt. The jeans were most comparable to a pair of buckskins, and they required no braces, but he felt strangely naked wearing the black shirt. It was tight enough to be glued to his body.

"I cannot go out wearing only an undershirt," he said, smoothing a hand down his stomach.

Rebecca stared at his stomach, swallowed hard, and then looked up at him. "I'm sorry, what?" she asked.

"This shirt," he repeated. "Surely this can't be all men wear? No waistcoat? No jacket? I feel it's too tight and small. Even if it did fit me better, I would feel bloody naked."

"Oh...yeah, no, it's fine. T-shirts are less bulky than whatever you're used to, but don't worry, you're fine now...I mean *it's* fine now...to wear...that shirt, I mean." She coughed and turned away to grab her little bag that looked like a lady's reticule and a set of keys. His lips quirked into a sly grin. Despite the modern age she lived in, Rebecca could be easily teased when it came to men and their lack of clothing. He would remember this for later...when he had time to find all the ways in which to give her pleasure.

"Come on." She opened the door and headed out. Devon reluctantly followed her. They were going to take the car. He *hated* the car. The shoes he had put on were a little too small, but he told himself it wouldn't be long before he got a proper pair that fit.

"I take it you have a modiste you visit regularly?" he asked as they climbed into the vehicle.

Rebecca leaned over to help him buckle a strap across his chest, which only reinforced his belief that this contraption was unsafe. "A what?"

The scent of her hair was sweet like fruit and flowers. He couldn't help but picture gripping this woman by the hair at the nape of her neck and kissing her until she was wet and moaning for him. She pulled away after a little click by his hip, and then she started the machine.

"What's a modiste?" she asked again.

"A modiste is a woman who makes clothes, a tailor of sorts. Young ladies always went to a modiste's shop to have their clothes made..." His voice trailed off, realizing that this too must have changed.

"Oh. We don't really have those anymore. I mean, I know some people still get their clothes tailored, but pretty much everyone just goes to the mall."

"The *mall?*" Devon mouthed the word, and it tasted foul in his mouth. It sounded common somehow. He didn't like the idea of doing what everyone else did. He was a rich man... Well, he *had* been.

"It's not so bad. We'll get in and get out really fast," she promised.

"*Humph.*" He frowned, watching the parade of endless vehicles around them as they drove to this "mall." It was going to be a bloody long day.

❦

REBECCA STARED AT THE CHANGING ROOM DOOR, waiting breathlessly to see if the clothes she'd picked for Devon worked out. She had to admit that dressing him was kind of fun, once she had convinced him that waistcoats and cravats were no longer considered everyday clothing.

He had a perfect body, like an underwear model. When he'd started to strip out of his clothes and failed to shut the door, three store attendants had lingered a little too long in the area, pretending to fold the same set of clothes over and over again. Rebecca had put a stop to it by hastily shutting the door herself. If ever a man had been invented by God to be catnip for women, it was Devon. With that gorgeous body and that sinfully wonderful accent, no woman would stand a chance. She wouldn't stand a chance if she wasn't careful.

Hold it together Rebecca. You can't go crushing on a guy who thinks he's from two hundred years ago. He needs help and don't forget, he probably stole the statue for which you're likely to get fired when your boss finds out.

"Ready?" she called out. He'd been in there for a long damn time.

"Er...I believe so," he replied and then opened the door. "You will have to tell me whether I'm presentable or not."

Her British hottie stood before her barefoot and in jeans that hugged his body just right, showing off his muscles but giving him room to move. He wore a white button-up shirt that clung to him but also wasn't too tight.

He ran a hand through his hair and glanced around nervously. "Well? Would you say I look presentable?"

There was a collective sigh behind Rebecca, and she turned to see the three female attendants staring at Devon with stars in their eyes. Not that she blamed them. Devon looked like a woman's wet dream. Just a hint of a bad boy by the way his shirt was unbuttoned at the top, and the way he filled out his jeans...

Damn.

She pictured him pinning her against the dressing room wall while fucking her into next Tuesday and watching their bodies in the mirror beneath the florescent lights. No one she'd ever dated had made her feel that hot and out of control.

She clenched her thighs, hating that she wanted this mentally unstable stranger so badly.

"Miss Clark?" Devon queried again. "Is this outfit suitable?"

"Yes, it is. And please, you need to call me Rebecca." Damn, her voice was too breathless.

He lifted a tie up. "I'm not sure what to do with this. I assume it's some sort of cravat, but..."

"Here, let me help." She came into the dressing room, and when she noticed the women still staring at him, she closed the door behind her. Her sudden awareness of Devon and being so close to him made her head spin. She flipped his shirt collar up and laid the tie around his neck. He kept his hands at his sides as he stared down at her hands, watching them perform the elaborate dance of loops and tugs that would create a Windsor knot. It was a good thing she'd grown up with a brother who had never bothered to learn how to do his own.

Devon raised his hands and put them on her waist. Her skin flushed with a responding heat.

"You're very good to me, Rebecca," he said. "To take me here, provide me with clothes..." One hand on her hip moved slowly around her body to touch the small of her back. Little sparks of heat burst outward from his touch.

"It's the right thing to do," she replied, her voice shaky as she tried to ignore the overwhelming wave of desire that spread through her body. God, she'd forgotten how good it felt to be close to a man, to feel his hands on her, even in a seemingly innocent touch. And Devon? He made her feel better than any man she'd ever been with. How was that possible? Just being there with her, talking to her, respecting her and thanking her for helping him? He'd been doing it all day and she never grew tired of his polite murmurs of thank you each time she taught him something new. A girl could get pretty spoiled with a man like that.

"Allow me to repay you." He lifted his other hand to brush a lock of hair back from her face. "You shouldn't hide your hair in a chignon," he said. Before she could stop him, he reached up and pulled the pencil out of her bun. Her hair tumbled down in messy waves around her shoulders.

"Oh! But—"

Her protest died on her lips as he ran his fingers through her hair, combing out the tangles.

He gripped her shoulders and turned her to face the mirror. "There, take a look."

She looked...gorgeous. The waves she'd always been afraid to let fall made her suddenly look sexy and wild in a way she'd never thought possible, especially with Devon there behind her watching her in the mirror.

"You should stop hiding your beauty. A man

cannot resist a woman like that," he whispered in her ear. She stared at their reflection. He was looking directly at her, not the mirror.

"Really?" She shouldn't have said that. It was a dangerous question because he could change his mind, say he wasn't interested in her. She wasn't prepared for that sort of rejection.

"Oh yes." The words were a low rumbling purr as he leaned down and cupped her face in his hands. She shivered and tried to back up but hit the wall of the changing room. He bit his lip as though trying to hide a smile, which only made him sexier.

Then he kissed her.

The sensation was an explosion of dark, forbidden tastes, like rich brandy and honeyed wine, things she'd never thought she'd taste on a man's lips. He kissed her like he had all the time in the world, time enough to explore her mouth and find out just what she liked.

Rebecca moaned against him. The way he touched her, with his featherlight kisses that turned deep and decadent, gave her a rush of wicked thoughts. When she opened her eyes, she saw his gaze rake down her body.

"You taste sweet, and it makes me think of a dozen things I could do to you right here." He trailed a line of kisses down her throat and brushed her hair back from her neck. He nipped her shoulder playfully, which set off little fireworks in her womb. She was afraid that the attendants outside would hear them. But if she was going to surrender to her fantasies, she wanted to know exactly what she was getting into.

"What sort of things?"

5

Devon spun Rebecca around so that she faced the wall and crowded her from behind.

"Did you know that I was considered quite the rake in my time?" he asked in a low voice.

Rebecca froze with a mix of fear and desire. "N-no..." She knew what a rake was supposed to be. A man who slept around, a ladies' man who knew the art of seduction. She was tempted and a little intimidated by the idea of being with someone like him.

"Quite irredeemable, they all said. A rogue, through and through." His hands molded to her loose blouse top, inching farther and farther up. Her skin burned deliciously in response. "But I can't say I ever encountered a woman who minded those qualities.

You asked what sort of things I would like to do to you. Shall I tell you? Shall I *show* you?"

Rational thought had left the station the moment he'd touched her, and she found herself saying, "Yes, *please*," without fully being aware of it.

"I would pull down these trousers of yours, for starters," he said as he nuzzled her ear. "And then I would touch you...here." He punctuated this statement by cupping her between her legs and pressing against her throbbing clit through her jeans.

Oh God, oh God, oh God, she silently chanted as her body spiked into a new level of arousal. An almost violent hunger overtook her. She *needed* him to touch her, to do everything his hands and words were promising. It had been so long since she'd had a fulfilling sexual encounter.

"Tell me...would you like that?" His voice teased her as he rubbed the heel of his hand against her mound.

"Yes!" she gasped. "God, yes!"

Someone pounded a fist on the changing room door. "Hey! This isn't a Motel 6!"

"Oh my—Let go! They can hear us!" Rebecca shoved Devon away, mortification suffocating her. They had been about to get busy in the changing room at the mall like a couple of horny teenagers!

What is the matter with me?

She knew the answer to that question. Devon. He

was walking catnip for women. His very touch was enough to drive her to do insane things...like jerk down her jeans and finger-fuck her with his hand. Oh yeah, that had almost happened, and she wasn't proud of it.

"What's wrong?" Devon asked, his eyes now clouded with concern. "Did I do something to upset you?"

She searched for her pencil on the floor but couldn't find it. It had to have rolled into another dressing room. She'd have to leave her hair down. Damn it.

"Rebecca." Devon caught her by the waist, forcing her to look at him when she still didn't answer him.

"We should get your clothes and leave, okay? Just finish putting on your socks and shoes and meet me at the cashier." She bolted from the room before she had a chance to think over how moronic she'd been, taking advantage of a delusional man who clearly had mental health issues.

She bumped into a woman as she was heading for the cashiers' counter.

"Sorry!" she gasped, but when she looked at the woman she froze.

This was no woman.

Or, it was, but it wasn't. Not really. There was something *more* about this person, a strange sort of beauty that didn't seem to be describable in normal words. A presence that didn't seem like it belonged in the same reality as hers. The world seemed to slow down, the customers, the TV screen over the cashiers showing off their products, everything, even her own breath became glacial.

"Rebecca," the woman said gently, her eyes the color of a summer sky. "You don't need to be afraid of Devon. He's exactly who he says he is. Do you understand?"

"What?" Rebecca stuttered.

"He's correct when he says it's my fault. Of course he deserved it, but I hadn't considered the added complications so much time passing would cause, how difficult it would be to make someone understand in this age of science. You see, I cursed him by turning him to stone, just like he said."

"Y-you..." Rebecca looked at the cashier as a woman seemed almost frozen in time handing over a credit card. *What's happening to me?*

"He was such a beautiful man—and a firecracker in the sack, as you say these days—but he had no regard for the satisfaction of his bed partner, and well, I couldn't let that go. Not when he left me wanting. Of course, it was his arrogance in not even *attempting* to make up for his behavior that truly angered me. I have a reputation to maintain, after all. So I cursed him."

She chuckled, the sound a mix between spring raindrops on glass and children humming songs. It was a glorious, intoxicating sound that made Rebecca forget she'd ever been upset or worried about *anything* in her life. It, more than anything else happening to her right now, convinced her of the reality of what the woman had just said.

"Devon is really two hundred years old?" she asked.

"He is."

Wow. Just wow.

"Promise me you will give him a chance?" the woman asked.

"A chance? For what?"

But the woman had vanished, people were moving again, and she was left standing next to a rack of jeans, apparently talking to herself. She glanced around, noticing some women staring at her.

"I'm having a mental breakdown. That must be it." She walked slowly to the cashier, her mind racing with everything the woman had just said. Devon wasn't crazy. He was from the 1800s, and a goddess really had cursed him into stone.

What was she going to do with *that* truth bomb?

IT WAS LATE AFTERNOON BY THE TIME THEY

returned to Rebecca's home, but Devon couldn't shake the feeling that something had happened to Rebecca after she'd left the changing room. She was quiet and answered his questions with as few words as possible. It put him on edge, making him feel as though something was off.

He'd carried the bags of his new clothes inside and set them down by the couch. As he sorted through them, he saw Rebecca pacing around the living room. She was talking into that little black thing she called a cell phone, and she sounded angry.

"Fine. I'll come in today, but I had asked for a day off. Yes...I understand. I'll be there in ten minutes. Yes... Right... Of course... But once I get things sorted out, I'm going home, okay?" She tossed the phone down on the couch and faced Devon.

"I've got to go back to work for a little bit and handle some things. I'd take you, but I'd really rather not have to explain you to everyone we run into. Can you stay here in the house while I'm gone?"

He didn't miss the note of pleading in her tone. "Of course. Evan and I shall stay right here, won't we, boy?" The terrier huffed in approval and nudged Devon's hand to encourage him to pet him.

"Thanks," Rebecca said. "Oh, you can walk him if he gets too hyper. His leash is by the door. The green one. Don't let him off the leash or he'll chase a squirrel or something and never come back. Just don't wander too far from the house, okay?"

She handed him a spare key, and in a matter of minutes, he and Evan were left all alone in the quiet little house.

"Would you like a walk?" he asked Evan. The dog barked and ran to the door, bouncing in excitement. He clawed at the door knob, something which he must have done frequently if the faint scratches in the wood around the knob were any indication.

"A walk it is, then." Devon removed the green leash from the peg on the wall and fixed it to Evan's leather collar.

The dog bounded down the street, dragging Devon behind him. It took quite a bit of concentration not to lose track of how to get back to the house. The streets were unlike anything he was used to, making it hard to remember landmarks to find his way back. They were gone for half an hour, and by the time they returned, Devon's arm ached from being pulled everywhere.

"Whoa, steady, boy," he commanded as they reached Rebecca's front lawn. He saw a flicker of movement from of the corner of his eye. He turned, but saw only a flash of white shifting back and forth in the windows of the house next door. Whatever strange slatted covering that blocked the window from the inside was moving, swaying back and forth.

Devon tilted his head, and Evan dropped down on his haunches to stare at the house as well.

"What do you think, boy?" he asked the dog. Evan whined and gazed up at him with soulful eyes.

With a sigh, Devon turned back to Rebecca's house, and they started up the paved walkway to her door.

"Excuse me!" An older woman's reedy voice cut through the afternoon birdsong.

He halted and saw a woman wearing a purple suit and strange white shoes leave the house he'd been staring at a moment ago.

"Can I help you, madam?" The woman had a thin face that was lined with wrinkles. Her brown hair was streaked with gray, and it was cut short and kept wavy, like a boy's.

"I'm Winifred Lesley, Rebecca's neighbor. I live there." The woman pointed to the house behind her.

"It's a pleasure to meet you, Mrs. Lesley." Devon bowed low, hoping that he was acting appropriately. This future was so full of...open familiarity with strangers, and he wasn't at all comfortable with it.

"I hate to be nosy... ah, who am I kidding? I live for it. But you see, I like Rebecca quite a bit, and I want to make sure that she's safe and taken care of." The woman stared at him, hands on her hips. "Now... are you her boyfriend? I haven't seen you around before."

"Boy...friend?" That was a curious word. "I'm not a boy, as you can see, but I do believe I am her friend," he replied, a little hesitant.

"You're certainly not a boy, heavens no." She gave a light chuckle, but then she seemed to recover her seriousness. "What I mean is, are you dating her? I don't want any young men sniffing around if they don't plan to stick around, you understand?"

Half of the woman's words made little sense, but Devon believed he understood the meaning she was trying to convey.

"You're trying to ascertain my intentions towards Rebecca?"

Winifred nodded.

"I assure you, my intentions are honorable. My only desire is to please her and take care of her." And it was the truth. He'd be cursed back into the stone if he didn't manage that. Therefore, his greatest desire was to give Rebecca everything she wanted and needed, hopefully in bed tonight, so he could prove to Aphrodite that he had learned his lesson.

"Good, good," Winifred said. "You should cook that girl a good meal. She's never had a decent man cook for her. I watch her, you see, through the windows. I've spent the last five years watching her slave away for all those men she's dated. Not one of them cleaned the house or cooked for her. I've done my best to scare those men off. She needs a *good* man."

Winifred was eyeing him critically again. He had the distinct feeling that she was measuring him against these past lovers, men who had clearly been fools.

What man wouldn't want to take care of Rebecca? She was sweet and kind, selfless in her giving. She'd fed him and let him stay in her home, even though it meant risking her reputation. And from the sound of it, she'd let other men mistreat her too. He wasn't one to volunteer himself for a servant's duty of cooking a meal, but he sensed that in this modern age that was something he would have to learn. So be it.

"Is that a common occurrence, madam? For young ladies of a marriageable age to allow men to mistreat them?" He hoped his question wouldn't sound too impertinent.

Winifred nodded. "Afraid so. Men these days don't respect women the way they used to. They want second mothers or some such, not partners in life. It's a shame. A good, smart girl like Rebecca should be with a good, attractive, and loving man. Instead, she gets pushed around by the men in her life, even that boss of hers at the museum. He's always making her give up her vacation days." Winifred shook her head. "Unpaid at that..."

An idea popped into Devon's head, but he was going to require some help.

"Mrs. Lesley, could I prevail upon you to assist me? I should very much like to prepare an evening meal for Rebecca, but I'm not sure how to do so in her kitchen."

The woman chuckled. "You're not the first man scared of the stovetop. I guess I could help. You have anything in the house worth cooking?"

He glanced back at the house. "I am not certain. I came from a family where we had servants prepare our meals."

Rebecca's neighbor chuckled. "So that explains it. The accent had me wondering. British, right?"

He nodded.

"From one of those rich families who live in a big house?"

Again, he nodded, relieved she understood.

"I've watched my fair share of *Downton Abbey*," the woman laughed. "And by that I mean I own them all on Blu-ray. Guess I'd better teach you to boil water and cook, hadn't I?" She started to march past him toward Rebecca's front door. She looked back and saw him standing there with Evan's leash, still trying to work out half of what she'd just said, and waved a hand at him. "Come on! We don't have all day! I assume you have the key?"

Evan gave a joyous bark and tugged on the leash.

Devon caught up to Winifred to open the door, and soon the unlikely pair were inside the kitchen.

"Now, first lesson, don't be afraid of the oven. It's not that complicated." Winifred gestured to the buttons. "You hit 'bake' to turn the oven on so it's ready to cook. Then you have to select the temperature. 375 degrees is a good start for most dishes but you can always look up recipes on Google."

"Google," he tested the word. That would have to be explained later.

"Right, Google is your friend. I can't tell you how many times I forgot the recipe for my favorite banana cake. All you have to do is look it up."

"Yes, of course," he agreed, even though he hadn't the faintest idea what she was talking about.

"Let's get some pans and cooking spray."

Devon watched Winifred whirl around the kitchen, opening cupboards and exploring drawers until she found the items she was searching for.

"Here we go..." She pointed at the counter full of cooking implements.

"Bloody hell," he muttered, completely overwhelmed.

"Oh hush, you'll be just fine. A little bit of cooking won't be that bad. I'll walk you through everything." Winifred grinned at him.

"Rebecca will be so impressed. Trust me, you want to impress her like this. Every woman just wants someone to take care of her now and then. And by cooking you'll prove you can."

"That is exactly what I desire." To care for Rebecca, even if he only had a week to do so, was something he wanted more than ever. He couldn't forget the loneliness he'd seen in her eyes so often. And the way she'd clung to Evan when she'd greeted him last night, as though he were a talisman she held up against the rest of the world to protect her. She must have suffered horribly at the hands of selfish men if Aphrodite had sent him to her of all women in this modern age. And after seeing her kindness, hearing her laugh and getting drunk on the sight of her smile, for the first time in his life, Devon wanted to do something for someone other than himself.

He was going to cook Rebecca a meal. It wasn't sex, but perhaps the goddess would understand that he was trying to help Rebecca in whatever way he could. And it sounded like she needed something else in her life aside from mind-blowing bed play. She needed a man who cared about her.

And I will be that man, Devon vowed.

❦ 6 ❧

It was nearly eight in the evening by the time Rebecca pulled up in the driveway. The crazy hours at work had almost made her forget the even crazier situation at home: the two-hundred-year-old man freed from stone. A man who was so innately sexy that she was having trouble focusing because her thoughts kept straying back to that kiss they'd shared and how it had made her feel alive again in a way she'd forgotten. This was how it started. Love. These warm, fuzzy, and spark-of-heat kind of feelings that left a woman breathless and dizzy.

You can't fall in love with him. You don't even know what will happen when his week is over and the goddess passes her judgment. He might be sent back in time and you'll never see him again.

There was a part of her that still didn't believe it, even though she had spoken directly to a goddess. *An actual goddess*. She parked her car and walked up to the front door, only to find it unlocked.

"Devon?" she called out. What if he'd gone somewhere and had gotten lost or hurt or...?

"In the kitchen," his deep voice answered. "Stay right where you are, if you please."

Sighing, Rebecca dropped her purse and briefcase on the floor, then leaned back against the door. Her feet ached from wearing heels all day. Usually she kicked off her shoes at the office, but her boss, Mr. Milliken, had made her follow him around for four hours, pointing out changes he wanted her to make in the new exhibitions. He was also the one who insisted that female employees wear skirts and heels. If Rebecca had her way, she'd ignore the damn dress code and wear pantsuits with flats.

Devon emerged from the kitchen wearing a pink apron with frilly lace, one her mother had given her as a joke for Christmas last year. She suppressed a giggle. "What are you wearing *that* for?"

"Hmm?" He glanced down, noticed the apron, and frowned. "Mrs. Lesley insisted that I should wear this. She also suggested I remove my shirt before you got home, but I didn't think that was a proper way to greet you. This is after all a lady's house, not a house of ill repute."

Rebecca tensed. "Wait, you let *Mrs. Lesley* in here?" That old woman was snooping in her house now?

"Er...yes. She's actually a rather charming lady—"

"Jesus, Devon, don't let her in here. She's always spying on me, judging me, and—"

He came and placed a fingertip on her lips. "Rebecca, that woman is a *genuinely* kind person. She hasn't been watching you. She's been watching *over* you. There's quite a difference. She told me about your former lovers and how they mistreated you. In fact, she interrogated me at length to ascertain whether or not I had honorable intentions. That woman is a friend to you and I suggest you treat her as such."

Devon's declaration gave her pause. Mrs. Lesley was looking out for her? She thought back on their encounters over the years. The way the older woman was always trying to talk to the boys she'd brought home for dates and how the really awful guys had been chased off almost at once because they didn't like Mrs. Lesley bothering them.

She'd been driving them away to help me?

That can't be. Huh. Then again...

Rebecca glanced toward the window above her sink where she knew she could see Mrs. Lesley's home if was stood in the kitchen. Had she misjudged the older woman all these years?

Devon was grinning again. "Now, cease your worrying. Mrs. Lesley assisted me this afternoon, and I do not want her efforts to go to waste. Close your eyes and follow me."

"Devon, what is all this?" she demanded, skeptical of whatever scheme he'd planned. Just because he was self-assured, that didn't mean he could be trusted to survive in this modern age. He was like a toddler in many ways. She couldn't forget how he'd reacted to the shower last night, or how he still didn't trust her cell phone when she showed him how she could talk to people.

"Are you ready for your surprise?"

"Uh...sure," she replied. Given the heavenly smells, she assumed he had gotten food into the house but he definitely couldn't have cooked anything. He didn't know how.

He brushed a lock of her hair back. Rebecca blushed when she realized he'd noticed she'd left her hair down ever since the department store. For a short time this afternoon she'd believed she could look beautiful and *feel* beautiful, and she didn't want to let that feeling go.

"Close your eyes and trust me." There was a hungry look in his eyes that her body echoed with a need of its own. But he didn't kiss her, didn't do any of the things that she was so close to begging him to do.

Because he doesn't want you as much as you want him. He's gorgeous. You've dated men like him before. They never care about women as much as they lead you to believe. He's just amusing himself by being nice to you.

It was a pattern she was all too familiar with, the shame of being left at a restaurant while her date chased down a cute, young waitress, or being completely stood up. Gorgeous hunks were always trouble, the first to break a girl's heart. But she wanted Devon to be different, so much so that it hurt.

She closed her eyes, and he took her hand. She followed cautiously as he led her toward the kitchen. When they passed the couch, she heard Evan's excited panting, but thankfully she didn't trip over him. Then, just as her heels hit the tile floor in the kitchen, the smells wafted even more strongly around her. Delicious, tantalizing smells. Her heart gave a wild thump, and she tried to calm down. When was the last time someone had cooked for her?

Never.

The answer burdened her with sadness, but she refused to let it taint this perfect moment. Devon ushered her into a seat at her little table.

"Can I open my eyes now?" she asked. There was a sound of clinking, then a *snick-snick* noise, and she felt a faint heat blossom close to her face.

"Yes," Devon announced.

Rebecca opened her eyes and stared in amazement at the perfectly set table, with candles that had just been lit. Devon walked over with two plates of spinach salad with freshly cut strawberries and mandarin slices, a light honey-based dressing, topped with crumbled feta and almond slivers.

"Wow," she whispered, staring at the salad.

Devon reached for a bottle of red wine and poured her a glass. "Please, start eating. I know you must be famished." He nodded at her plate, and she couldn't resist diving in. The salad was amazing, light but tasty. He removed his apron and set it on the counter before he took a seat to eat his own dinner.

"I've also prepared some chicken and scalloped potatoes." Devon took a sip of his wine, his eyes hopeful, yet also full of personal pride.

"Seriously?" Rebecca stared at him. "When did you learn to...? I mean, you didn't know how to use the oven or..."

"Mrs. Lesley was most instructive. I had to take copious notes on how all the buttons worked and what temperatures to cook at, but I believe I have mastered the fundamentals." He grinned. "I assume, by the look you walked in with, that you've had a challenging day at your job?"

Rebecca blew out a breath. "You could say that. My boss is an OCD nut job who wants to change everything to make it perfect. But it already is perfect, you know? And I had to keep distracting him so he didn't go into the wing where the statue...er... you were, I mean. If he finds that gone, I'm toast. I convinced the janitors to put up some cleaning signs. It can buy a few days, but he'll want to see it soon to prepare it for the new exhibit launch, and then I'm out of a job." She rubbed at her temples, massaging them as Devon finished his salad before she took another gulp of wine.

"I'm sorry," Devon said with a sigh. "Perhaps the goddess will grant you a boon and handle that pathetic excuse for a man."

She laughed, picturing an angry goddess turning him into the missing marble statue.

"If I might ask, what is OCD?"

"Obsessive-compulsive disorder. It's a condition people have where they need to have everything perfect, and they get a little crazy about it."

Devon chuckled. "In my day, we simply called those people *mothers*." He was smiling, but the smile faded and his gaze darkened.

Rebecca didn't like seeing shadows in his eyes. "What's the matter?"

"I..." He cleared his throat. "It's nothing. Please, tell me more about your day."

Rebecca realized what he was trying to do. Be the

perfect man. Make her dinner, ask her about her day...
But she didn't need him to be perfect.

"Devon, please, talk to me." She reached across
the table and took his hand in hers, squeezing it.
"What's wrong?"

He hesitated, looking at their connected hands.

"I just realized that after two centuries in stone,
everyone I ever loved is...gone. I hadn't thought of
that before now. I was so angry at Aphrodite for trap-
ping me that I hadn't thought about anyone else, not
even my own family. My mother and my two younger
brothers are..." He didn't say the word *dead*, but it
lingered in the air between them.

"Oh, Devon, I'm so sorry." Her response felt
weak, but she didn't know how to comfort a man
who'd lived two hundred years ago.

The pain in his eyes vanished as he dropped a
shield over his heart. She could see it happening, the
shuttering of his emotions until there was only a
pleasant and controlled smile upon his face. It left
her feeling dismissed and confused.

"Ready for the second course?" He rose and went
to the oven, using mitts to pull out the chicken and
potatoes.

They ate in silence. She was glad for that because
she was starving, but she also didn't know what else
to say.

"Do you enjoy dancing?" Devon suddenly asked.

"Dancing?"

"Yes. You know, waltzing, quadrilles..."

"Er... I only know the waltz, but people don't really dance that way anymore. We just sort of slow dance."

"Slow...dance?" He drew out the words, as though testing them to see if that would reveal their meaning. "Do you mean the music is played slower?"

"Sort of. It's...well, it's not hard." She wasn't a fantastic dancer, but everyone could slow dance.

"Would you teach me?" he asked. A longing had softened his eyes again, and she couldn't resist.

"Sure."

"Wonderful! I've missed dancing," he admitted as he finished his dinner. He collected their plates, cleaned them, and set them inside the dishwasher. Rebecca stared at him in awe. Cooking and now the dishes? *And he wants me to teach him to slow dance.* Aphrodite had made a mistake turning this man into stone. Rebecca had never been able to get any of her old boyfriends to dance with her.

Rebecca went into the living room and glanced around. There was probably enough room in the backyard to dance, but not inside.

"Let's go outside." She stood in her heels and winced.

"Are you all right?" He touched her gently on the

hip as they slipped out the back door and stood on the small brick patio.

"Oh, I'm fine. My feet just hurt after wearing these damned heels all afternoon." She gave a little kick of her right foot, showing the high heel.

"Women in my day usually wore slippers and the occasional boot with heels if they were going outdoors, but those heels were much shorter."

"Lucky them," Rebecca said with a sigh. Then she squeaked in surprise as she was hoisted in the air and carried to a lawn chair, where she was set back down. Devon knelt at her feet and gently took the high heels off, rubbing her tender soles with his hands.

"Better?"

The only sound that escaped her was a mix between a sigh and a moan as he continued to rub her aching feet.

"You have to stop doing that," she said.

"Doing what?" he asked as he looked up into her eyes.

"Er...nothing." She hastily got to her feet and then held out a hand. "You wanted to learn to slow dance, remember?"

"Yes, if you still want to teach me." He glanced down at her feet with hesitation.

"I do." The thought of showing him how to dance slow, their bodies close, was too tempting to resist.

The night air around them quieted down except for the occasional coo of doves and chirp of crickets.

He took her hand, and she pulled him into the center of the patio, then faced him.

"First, I put my hands around your neck," she said, sliding her arms up until she locked her fingers at the nape of his neck. "Then you put your hands on my waist." When his palms curled around her waist, she shivered, relishing how good it felt.

Devon lowered his head so their faces were impossibly close. "And then?"

"Then we move together, a step to my left as you take a step to your right. You move slightly forward, and I move back at the same time."

"That's all?"

"That's all."

His large hands were on her hips, making her feel delightfully feminine. Her tweed skirt, which flared at her knees, swayed as they began to dance.

"How am I doing?" he asked, moving his face closer until their cheeks pressed together.

"Wonderful." *Simply wonderful.*

She shifted, leaning against his shoulder, and she felt him rest his head on top of hers as they continued to slowly glide around the patio. They danced as though in a dream—*her* dream.

"I like this much better than waltzing," he whispered.

She couldn't help but smile. "Do you?"

"Yes. In my day, waltzing was as close as we could get to a woman in public, and even then it could be considered scandalous." He rubbed her waist with one hand. "Dancing so close as we are now, it would be considered compromising."

"How compromising?"

"We'd have to marry to save your reputation." He chuckled, but his tone was strange, as though he thought the idea was not silly at all, but rather intriguing. It reminded Rebecca of how different their worlds were, how much had changed in two hundred years.

She had a million questions for him, but she knew if she asked them, the answers might make things awkward. Well, *more* awkward. But she had to know.

"Devon, did you love someone before...well, before you were turned into stone?" She couldn't imagine a man like him not loving someone.

She lifted her head from his shoulder to gaze into his eyes. There were faint lines around them, as though he'd smiled a lot. But he wasn't smiling now.

"I have never been fortunate enough to love a woman. I've made love to many, but *love* was not a concern of mine then. It was part of the reason I was cursed. For being a selfish bastard." He closed his eyes a moment, sighing before he opened them again.

"You're cold. We should go back inside. I have dessert waiting."

He stepped away, and the distance between them seemed to span centuries rather than feet. It shouldn't have left an ache in her chest, but it did.

We're from different worlds. Different times.

❧ 7 ❧

Devon returned to the kitchen, his pulse racing. Dancing with Rebecca had begun a stirring inside his heart, a heart he'd feared had remained stone even when Aphrodite had turned him back to flesh and blood. A stirring like the first tentative shoots of flowers in early spring. A promise of things to come, of things to change.

Am I capable of change? After spending the last two centuries caged in stone with no hope of escape or death, he'd had no thoughts of change, only survival or death. But he was free now, free in a way he'd never imaged and he was here with a woman unlike any he'd ever met before.

He'd learned more about her today while they'd shopped and spent time together than he ever had another soul. She was a woman who loved walking in the morning and seeing the sunrise crest the trees with its brilliant splash of colors. She had ambitions someday to run a museum, and she was obsessed with art, especially sculptures. Her brilliant mind left him spinning in wonder. He found it so easy to talk with her, to tell her about his own life, the parts that he wasn't ashamed of, and every moment with her felt like a precious grain of sand slipping into an hour-glass. He didn't want to think about when the week was up and what the goddess would do with him then.

Rebecca's voice came from behind him. "Devon, I'm sorry if I did or said something that upset you." He turned to face her. Her lips trembled, and her eyes brimmed with tears that she was doing her best to pretend weren't there. The hardness of his heart fractured, creating a great spider web of cracks that spread across the walls he'd built up for so long. The beating heart he'd spent years ignoring was burning for her in a way he barely understood. But the feeling of lightness inside him, the burdens of his past sins, seemed to fade whenever Rebecca was near him.

"You didn't. You could never upset me," he said in a low, husky tone. She met his gaze as he closed the distance between them, and he saw a spark of brilliant lightning in her eyes, an energy that called out to him like the sweet song of a siren on distant rocks in a stormy sea. After two centuries without a woman in his arms, he was done waiting, done playing by a fickle goddess's rules.

He raised a hand to cup Rebecca's cheek and slanted his mouth over hers. He explored her lips, learning the shape and feel of them in a way he had only imagined during his long imprisonment. Before this moment, his kisses had been frivolous, a playful game that had teased with promises. The time for teasing was over. He *wanted* her, and he was done playing the gentleman.

With each press of his lips, he stoked the fire inside her into something hotter. Devon pulled her into his arms, and she responded. Her mouth on his sent spirals of hunger through him. He needed more. With a soft growl, he lifted her into the cradle of his arms and carried her through the kitchen and up the stairs to her bedroom. She broke the kiss, panting softly against his neck.

"Devon, what are we—?"

He hushed her with a kiss as he set her on the edge of her bed, then leaned over and captured her mouth again, cupping her face and reveling in the warm velvety touch of her lips. A whimper of need escaped her as he reached for the buttons of her tweed vest. Her hands grasped his wrists, stopping him.

"Wait," she gasped, and he stepped back. His body tensed as he tried to calm himself. If she wanted to stop, he would, but by God he prayed she didn't want to. "I can do it much faster," she said, her fingers nimbly slipping buttons through their slits until she'd cast the vest aside. Then she was pulling her white blouse out of her skirt and unbuttoning it as well.

Devon removed his black T-shirt but didn't touch his jeans—that would only come after he'd pleasured her to her satisfaction. He wanted to see the tightly wound Rebecca flat on her back, spent and exhausted with glorious ecstasy before he took her. He'd had a lot of time to ponder why Aphrodite had been so angry with him, and perhaps ironically the endless thoughts of what he should have done long ago now only fueled his libido.

"God you're beautiful," she whispered as she reached up to touch his bare chest.

He chuckled. "You are the beautiful one." He slipped his fingers through the lacy straps of her black... What manner of stays were these? He'd never seen a contraption like it before. It was too small to properly cover a woman; rather, it lifted her breasts up and presented them for his hands and mouth, yet did nothing to hide her glorious breasts. Whoever had invented this bit of cloth had his eternal gratitude. He knelt in front of her and studied her skirt, wondering how best to get it off.

"It has a zipper. You just pull on the little metal

thing and it undoes itself in the back," she said, her voice breathless. She rolled onto her side, trying to show him the zipper.

"Ahh! I see! The same as on my jeans," he laughed softly in delight. Before she could react, he'd gotten to his feet, flipped her onto her stomach, and unzipped the skirt, tugging it down. She gave a little squeal as he then flipped her onto her back again.

"Devon!" She placed her palms flat on his chest, and he towered over her at the edge of the bed.

"Do you wish for me to stop?"

"No...just give me a minute, okay? It's been a while since I've done this." Even though it was fairly dark in the room, with evening shadows stretching through the windows, he could see the blush on her face spreading down to her collarbone. His chest tightened and he smiled, stroking her lips with his fingers.

"It will be all right, love. I'll go as slow as you desire," he vowed, even if it would kill him. He didn't want her nervous or afraid—he wanted her wild and excited. If it took hours to reassure her, then so be it. He would take all the time required for her to trust him. He'd been a masterful lover once. But by that fateful with night Aphrodite he'd grown careless and lazy when it came to women and she had rightfully cursed him. Two hundred years in stone had changed some things inside him, but the old lover was still there, a man who knew how to please his woman. The difference now was his priorities—pleasing Rebecca instead of himself.

He bent over her and kissed his way down from her lips to her breasts, tugging the lacy cups down to free her tempting breasts. Her nipples pebbled against the cold air, but he covered one with his hand and the other with his mouth. Rebecca moaned and arched back. He chuckled as her hands dug into his hair, holding him to her breasts.

"God, *Devon*..."

"I'm just getting started." He tugged the lacy scrap of cloth from her hips, baring her completely. Then he knelt again in front of the bed and wedged his shoulders between her thighs.

She gasped, trying to sit up. "Wait—what?" Clearly she was not expecting what he had planned.

"Lie back and enjoy, love," he commanded.

"O-okay." She lay back down, and a thrill rippled through him at this little victory. Devon placed a kiss on her inner right thigh, then her left, before he used his fingers to stroke her folds. She was wet and hot, and it was going to drive him mad to wait to sate his needs, but he wanted her to experience what he could do with this mouth.

He kissed the top of her mound, letting her feel his tongue flick against the small bud of arousal, and she let out a keening whimper. From that moment on, he showed her how much he wanted her to enjoy what he could give her.

She climaxed twice, her sweet taste upon his tongue, her trembling legs against his shoulders, and her gasping words of ecstasy in his ears as she came down from those glorious heights of pleasure. The evening light illuminated her like pale alabaster with only a hint of rose, and he had never seen anything more glorious in his life.

And she is mine. In this moment, I own every part of her.

He rose, his hands fumbling for the buttons of his jeans, his breath coming fast as he realized he was going to bed a woman, something he hadn't done in two hundred long years.

"Devon." Rebecca's voice caressed his name, and he froze as another voice, one that filled him with dread shook him deep inside like thunder.

"Be careful Devon...Your time of sacrifice has not yet passed." The echo of Aphrodite's laughter clung to the air like a hint of perfume, faded and invisible but still there.

He dropped his hands from his jeans and stepped away from the bed, away from Rebecca. How could he have forgotten his vow to Aphrodite? He had seen to her pleasure, yes, but the deity's terms now came back to his mind, haunting him. The devil is in the details, they say, and with a scorned goddess this was doubly so. He could not sate himself, could not enjoy Rebecca as he would have any other woman. Not if he wished to remain in the world of the living.

His shoulders went rigid as he fought to regain control. His body surged with unsatisfied hungers, and he struggled to bury them.

Rebecca sat up, her hair falling down around her shoulders, covering her breasts before she raised her hands to shield her body. "What's wrong?"

"I..." Words failed him when they never had before. "I cannot do this."

He grabbed his abandoned shirt from the floor and stumbled from the room. If he stayed close to her, naked and beautiful as the morning sun on snow in winter, the desire would bloody well damn him for all eternity.

<hr />

REBECCA DIDN'T CHASE AFTER HIM. THAT WAS something the old Rebecca would have done. She would have gone after him and demanded answers, only to be disappointed and get her heart broken. She was done being that sort of woman.

Devon had opened up a new side of her. She'd gotten a taste of what she'd wanted from life, from a relationship, and she wasn't going to allow anyone to mistreat her again. Whatever had happened between them tonight had scared him off, that much was clear, but she wasn't going to blame herself. Still, his rejection didn't hurt any less no matter what she told herself. She got out of bed, took her robe from her closet, and headed for the shower.

The hot water beating against her skin was a blessed relief. She leaned against the back of the shower wall and closed her eyes.

I have a two-hundred-year-old, gorgeous, sexy-as-hell man in my house thanks to an ancient Greek goddess. I'm living in a world where I can't have the one thing I want— his heart.

Rebecca blinked away the tears in her eyes. Wait, she wanted his heart? They'd only known each other a short time, and she stoutly did *not* believe in love at first sight. Yet, she couldn't deny that she felt *something* for him, something that ran deep, like still waters in a vast lake. But she was afraid to face those feelings and the uncertainty of the future.

What if he ended up being like every guy she'd dated before? Arrogant, selfish, and incapable of loving a woman while still respecting her as an equal partner. Hell, it was the reason he'd been imprisoned in stone in the first place! She wasn't a maid or a chef on call. She had a full-time career that had stresses, worries, and complications, just like every other person. She hadn't met a man yet who'd truly understood that.

Which is probably why I'll die alone.

The sobering thought threatened to start a fresh wave of tears. Rebecca buried her face back beneath the spray, wanting to hide in the hot, steamy glass box forever. But she couldn't do that. She had to get out, even if it was the last thing in the world she wanted to do.

With a weary sigh, she turned off the water and reached for her towel. She yelped when she realized Devon was standing there, still bare-chested and wearing nothing but his jeans, watching her with hooded eyes.

"I upset you." His voice was ragged as emotion tore through his voice. "I'm sorry. I never wanted that. I never wanted to hurt you."

Rebecca's throat constricted. "I wasn't…" The lie burned bitterly upon her lips.

"I wish I could undo the hurt I caused, but I cannot. The fault is mine." His throat worked as he struggled to continue. "Aphrodite cursed me."

"I know," she replied, clutching the towel over her body.

"But you do not know the *conditions* she placed upon me." His blue eyes burned with fury, but Rebecca wasn't afraid.

"Conditions?"

He stepped closer but still kept his distance. "I have seven days to prove that I can put a woman's desires above my own. If I were to seek out my own satisfaction, even after you reaching yours, I have no doubt that I would be turned back into stone." He looked over her body, and she could feel it, almost as though he'd caressed her. "We came too close in your bedchamber. I almost lost control and took you the way I wanted, the way I *craved*..."

It all made sense now, and Rebecca exhaled, her lungs burning. She hadn't even realized she'd been holding her breath while he spoke.

"You mean you can't...*finish*?"

"Yes." He came to her then, towering over her as he cupped her face in his hands. Their mouths were only inches apart, and she could see into his eyes. For a moment she thought she glimpsed his very soul. The shifting glints of light fused with desire melded with something deeper, something more pure, and it left her breathless.

"You were such a temptation that I would have damned myself for all eternity to have but one moment with you." And then he kissed her.

It was a kiss made of dreams and starlight that spun her world in a dizzying array of colors and sensations. His warm body, the feel of his arms as he slid them around her. The taste of her own tears mixed with a hint of his sweetness upon their lips. The devastating perfection of that single, fleeting, yet somehow everlasting kiss was imprinted upon her soul.

There would be no other man who would hold her heart captive as he did in that moment.

We're both cursed.

"What are we going to do?" she asked as they broke apart.

He rubbed his hands up and down her back. "Try to survive six more days." Both of them were afraid to ask the question: What would happen when those six days had come and gone?

8

Six days might as well have been an eternity for Rebecca. It was wearing on Devon too. They spent each evening together, laughing, cooking, dancing on the patio after dinner. Each night, he would walk her to her bedroom, pull her into his arms, and kiss her tenderly. But it could never lead to more, and it was killing her. After nearly losing control the first time, they'd agreed not to go to bed together, even for just her pleasure. It was too much of a risk and she didn't want anything to happen to him because she couldn't resist temptation.

On the evening of the sixth day, Rebecca lingered by the kitchen, watching Devon do the dishes. He was still amused by the novelty of putting dirty dishes into a the dishwasher rack and turning it on, then allowing the machine to do the rest. Rebecca couldn't help but stare at those jeans that hugged his ass. The man was temptation wrapped in sin and coated with desire, and she wanted him more than she wanted *anything* in her life.

"Devon." She spoke his name softly.

He turned, dark hair falling into his eyes. "Yes?"

"Tonight at midnight will be seven days. You've given me everything I've desired. Aphrodite would have to agree, right? Do you think we could...?" She couldn't resist smiling when understanding glinted in his eyes.

"I would like nothing more." But his smile faltered. "Aphrodite?" he called out.

Silence was their only answer, and he sighed.

Rebecca looked around the room. "Maybe she can hear us anyway? I can't imagine she's forgotten about you."

Devon spoke louder. "Goddess! Have I passed your test? Is Rebecca's request something I may grant after midnight?"

Again silence. Then the doorbell rang.

Rebecca frowned as she left the kitchen to go answer the door. "Who could that be?" Devon followed her, the heat of his body warm behind her as she opened the door and he put a hand on her waist. No one was there.

Devon looked over her shoulder and pointed

down at the doormat. "What's that?" Rebecca picked up a small gift bag and dug through the tissue paper, finding a box of extra-large condoms.

"What are those?" Devon picked up the box, studying it with interest as he mouthed the words "ribbed for her pleasure" written on the side.

"Oh God!" She grabbed him and dragged him and the bag back inside the house, slamming the door.

"There's a note." Devon turned the box over, where a little white card was taped to the side. He opened it and read it aloud. "At midnight, you are free. But not a moment before. Enjoy this little gift. —A."

"The goddess of love sent us a box of condoms?" Rebecca's cheeks burned with embarrassment, but she was also on the verge of laughing.

"What are con—doms? It sounds familiar." Devon tested the word, smiling as he seemed to notice her blushing.

"They're um...here." She smacked the box against his chest and fled back to the kitchen. He was a man —he could figure it out.

She busied herself with pouring two glasses of wine, and when she looked up, he'd entered the kitchen, grinning as he waved the box of absurdly large condoms in his hands.

"Ah, now I remember. They were more commonly referred to as French letters in my day." He studied the box intently. "Are they still made of sheep intestines?"

"Sheep intestines?" Rebecca echoed faintly. *Oh holy mother of—* "No, they use latex. It's not made from any part of an animal."

"Latex?"

"Thin rubbery mat...oh, never mind. It's better, trust me."

Devon chuckled. "What luck! I always hated using them. A man had to soak them in a jar for hours before he could get them on. Terribly messy things."

The mental image made her wince. *Talk about an ick factor.*

"Let's not talk about old-fashioned condoms anymore, okay? In fact, let's not talk about any of them again until we get a chance to use them." She took the box from his hand, opened a cupboard, and shoved them inside.

She turned back to Devon. He had his arms crossed and was biting his lip as though to keep from laughing. "I do love how modest you are, but come midnight, I want the *other* Rebecca, the one who will scream my name." His voice had turned husky. "Because I wish to be inside you until dawn, giving you pleasure over and over until you cannot leave the bed because you're drunk with ecstasy."

Her mouth ran dry, and she struggled to think coherently past the explosion of heat inside her. The thought of making love with him for *hours*, from midnight to dawn? To think about him making her come over and over...

Rebecca gripped the shreds of her self-control. She had to find a way to distract them both before midnight.

"We still have four hours. Why don't we find something safe to do far away from my bed?" She handed him a glass of wine and then took a sip of her own. "And I have an idea."

❧

THE INTERNET WAS A MOST FASCINATING THING, Devon decided. Any question he'd ever had could be answered in seconds. The mysterious Google that Mrs. Lesley had told him about turned out to be something Rebecca had called a search engine. You could put any question in the box and it would provide a hundred answers.

He and Rebecca settled down on the couch with an object she called a laptop, probably because it sat on her lap. It had a flat glimmering face that she could make change instantly, much like the TV and cell phone.

"Look." She pointed at what she'd called the screen, and he read the words "Ancestry Registry" with a picture of a tree, the leaves and branches slowly growing.

"What is this?" he asked, peering closer.

"I thought we could research your family, find out what happened to them." She watched him hesitantly, as though she was afraid it might upset him.

His throat tightened, and he nodded. "Thank you, Rebecca. I mean that, from the bottom of my heart." He watched her as she filled out the various forms on the screen, and it asked him questions about his ancestry.

In a short time she beamed at him, tapping her fingers on the little square at the base of her laptop. "Yes! We found them! Your family is still around." She zoomed in on a large tree structure that had leaves with names and dates on them. His brothers, Rhys and Colin, were there, the branches splitting down over the years until they reached their modern-day descendants. The title was still in the family name, it seemed, with the oldest male son directly from Rhys's bloodline.

Rebecca nestled back against him, and he could see her face reflected on the screen. "It looks like both your brothers married and had long lives with lots of kids." She looked happy, but there was a wistfulness about her eyes and mouth, as though something she desired was not quite within her reach.

In that moment he felt the same. Neither he nor Rebecca had asked the goddess the one question that haunted them both. After midnight, what would she do with him? Would she leave him here in an era that wasn't his? Would she return him to the past? He closed his eyes and held Rebecca close, nuzzling her cheek. She murmured something so softly that he didn't hear what she said until she was tugging on his shirt.

"It's half an hour till midnight," she said, turning in his arms.

"I'm quite aware," he murmured back, smiling down at her. He didn't want to move from here, from this moment. The woman of his dreams, the woman he'd never known he should have been searching for in his life, was right here where she belonged.

He lowered his head again and pressed his lips to hers in a slow kiss. He took his time, feathering her lips with his, teasing her with the tip of his tongue before she opened her mouth and he took possession of it. Rebecca moved the laptop onto the table so she could crawl onto his lap, straddling him on the couch.

He gripped her jean-clad arse, loving how her bottom filled his hands. Bless the man who had decided women should wear pants. It was far more arousing than a mess of skirts and petticoats. She could ride his body just like this, torturing them both with the pleasure that would come just after midnight. He pulled her tighter to him, letting her slid up his body and back down as they kissed, mimicking penetration until his body was hard and aching but he didn't want to stop. It felt too good. Devon gripped her back, fisting one hand in her hair so he could pull her head back slightly and leave little kisses on her neck and throat.

"How do you know just what to do? It's like you... are perfect." Rebecca moaned, squirming on his lap.

"I spent years perfecting my technique," he whispered before biting her earlobe and she whimpered, grinding her pelvis harder against his. She gripped his shoulders, digging her nails in.

"Come upstairs with me," she begged. "We can do everything but...you know...until midnight."

"So modest, Lord, you are the sweetest creature," Devon chuckled and kissed her again, his mouth rougher as he couldn't help but picture finally claiming her as his, possessing her in the most primal way.

She climbed off the couch and he wanted to protest.

"Let's go, show me how bad a rogue you were." She winked at him and he laughed. She had no idea how bad he could be...

"Very well, I'm more than happy to provide a demonstration of my skills," he wiggled his fingers in the air and she laughed.

They headed silently upstairs, but he froze as he realized they were missing one crucial thing. He rushed into the kitchen and grabbed the box of condoms from the cupboard. When she saw what he was carrying, she grinned.

"Race you!" She challenged.

He darted up the stairs after her, laughing as he caught her by the waist as they reached the bedroom. He set the condoms down and she opened the box, pulling a small flat packet from it and setting it on the bed.

She turned back to him. "We'll get to that later, but first..." She curled her arms around his neck and kissed him. He took his time, learning her lips all over again as though he'd never get another chance. The lingering shadow of worry that this could be his one and only chance to make love to Rebecca filled him with a bittersweetness he'd never felt before. He threaded his fingers through her hair, reveling in the silky texture and the floral scent that clung to the strands.

They stripped out of their clothes, leaving a pile on the floor beside the bed.

"What time is it?" he asked between their fevered kisses. They lay close together, holding each other, their bodies fully skin to skin for the first time. She looked at the clock by her bed.

"Still fifteen minutes to go," she whispered, stroking her hands down his arms and back.

He felt dizzy with the strength of his desire for

her. What would it be like to see her come apart in his arms while he was inside her? Being with a woman had never felt so intense before. Certainly it had always been a delightful pleasure to indulge in, but now it felt like so much more. Everything was magnified a thousand times because he knew this woman, knew her dreams, her hopes, her deepest desires. In more ways than he could imagine, he felt she was an equal, not like the pretty young ladies from his time. None of them compared to this beautiful, complicated, perfect woman.

"Then I know just how to spend that time." He pushed her back on the bed, parting her thighs so he could gaze down at her. She blushed a dark red and closed her eyes.

"Look at me, darling," he growled softly as he pressed a kiss to her inner thigh. She lifted her head and stared down the length of her body at him. He knelt between her thighs and kissed a slow trail down to her mound. Her belly quivered.

"I don't think I could stand it if you did...that... again," she panted.

"Oh, you can, my love, you can," he promised. Then he inserted two fingers into her, stretching her. Lord she was so hot and tight, it made his cock ache, but he pushed down his own feelings and focused only on her. He stroked inside her, and she hissed as he found a hidden spot of pleasure.

"Oh God!" She arched her back, trying to escape his hold, but he gripped her waist with one hand.

"Feel that?" he murmured. "Right there?" he stroked the spot with the tips of his two fingers again and again until she cried out and went limp beneath him. Then he withdrew his fingers and licked them. She watched him through hooded eyes, shuddering a little.

"You're the devil," she laughed, shakily, her body still trembling with aftershocks.

"I do love to indulge in sinful behavior," he agreed with a knowing smirk and then he lowered his mouth to her folds which glistened with her desire.

"You're going to kill me!" she tried to buck her hips but he held her down as he feasted upon her, licking her until she couldn't breathe.

Only after she'd come apart again did he finally relent and let her rest for a moment. He sat back on his heels at the foot of the bed, watching her beautiful body bare and waiting for him. She was stretched out like a woman ready to be sacrificed to a lusty god and he wanted to be that god who claimed her body, taking pleasure and more importantly giving pleasure right back to her. He finally understood now what it meant to care about someone else, not just in bed. He'd spent all week thinking of ways to please her, from washing the car, to dishes, to cutting flowers from Mrs. Lesley's flower beds and forming lovely bouquets. The hard work was worth it to see her smile, and each time he saw that expression on her face it hit him hard right behind his knees.

Rebecca struggled to sit up, face flushed and hair adorably mussed as she curled her arms around him and slid into his embrace.

"It's one minute past midnight." Rebecca nibbled his ear, and a bolt of fresh arousal shot clear through him.

One minute passed. He was safe, he could give his woman what she wanted and find his own pleasure with her at last.

"Thank God!" They reached for the shiny packet at the same time, and she tore it open with her teeth. Then she removed the condom and pushed him onto his back. He watched as she showed him how to roll it over his hardened shaft. Far better than a sheep's intestine, to be sure. She was skillful and seductive, batting her dark lashes as she stroked him.

"You're killing me!" he gasped. Before he could stop to think, he switched their bodies so she lay beneath him, her legs parted, and he settled into the cradle of her thighs.

"Are you ready?" he asked, nuzzling her throat.

"I've been ready for six days." Her giggle turned into a moan as he thrust into her. He made sure she didn't have breath for anything more than soft, languid sighs and hushed moans of encouragement as he rode her. He clasped her hands in his and pressed their joined hands into the mattress on either side of her head as he showed her just how good a lover he really was.

As she came apart a minute later, he groaned and felt himself explode apart. It was too intense, too glorious—

Then a violent pain struck him, and he rolled off Rebecca, coughing as he fell off the side of the bed. Thunder crashed outside, and an angry voice filled the room.

"You had your chance, Devon Blake, and you had but a few minutes more before I would set you free. Now you face eternity in stone."

White light blinded his eyes as he struggled to get up on one knee. Everything went dark and cold... stone cold.

For a long moment Rebecca couldn't move. She stared at the statue of Devon on one knee, one hand raised above his eyes as though to shield himself from a bright light no one else could see.

"But we *waited*! Aphrodite, we waited until after midnight!" she shouted at the ceiling, her heart breaking as she tried to understand what was happening.

"No. It has only just now turned midnight." A woman appeared in the corner of the room, dressed in a black cocktail dress with killer red heels. It looked as though Aphrodite had just popped in from some fancy party.

Rebecca pointed at her nightstand. "Look! It's ten minutes past."

The goddess shook her head, the honey-colored ringlets of her hair bouncing around her shoulders.

"You humans have always believed you could bend the universe to your will. Do you think that when you travel through a time zone a whole hour magically jumps by? Or that these zones conform to the shape of your states and countries? As far as this planet is concerned, your clock is fast by ten minutes."

Rebecca's head spun. "But I made him—it was my fault. We thought it was midnight." She got out of the bed, clutching the sheet around her like a toga.

"That is not my concern. My terms were very specific."

"But you're a goddess. Can't you change your mind? Please?"

Aphrodite raised one eyebrow, coolly watching her. "And why should I do that? What is so special about Devon that he deserves my mercy a second time?"

Rebecca stared at Devon's stone body, and her eyes filled with tears. "I thought you were the goddess of love. How does this serve love? I have been looking for love, for the perfect man, the perfect relationship. I'd given up, but then you sent *him* to me."

She tried to still her racing heart as she sought the right words. "I didn't want to give him a chance until you told me his story was true. But he showed me what was in his heart. He showed me that there is a man out there who is perfect for me. And I don't mean he did everything right all the time. I mean that he treated me the way I wanted to be treated, as a woman worthy of love and respect. As an equal. He gave me my sense of value back. He gave me *love*. That was my greatest desire. My only desire. Surely you out of everyone should know how much that matters?" She kept her gaze fixed on the goddess.

Aphrodite considered this, though she seemed far from convinced. "The gods all have rules. Rules which must be followed. The conditions of his release were broken, but the fault was not Devon Blake's. It was yours. Therefore, if I show mercy, it will be to send him back to his time, not to stay here with you. Is that what you want?"

Rebecca swallowed and stared at the statue of Devon. She'd lose him forever regardless, but only one choice would give him a chance at life again.

"Yes. Please. Give him his life back."

Aphrodite sighed. "Very well. In the name of love, I shall return him." She snapped her fingers, and both the statue and the goddess vanished. The final beating pieces of Rebecca's heart turned to dust.

❧ 9 ❦

London—September 1816

Devon stumbled through the gardens, his heart pounding as he struggled to catch his breath. The muted sounds of laughter and fireworks that blossomed in the sky overhead were all too familiar.

"I'm...home..." The words escaped his lips in a ragged whisper. He was home, but he wasn't with Rebecca.

"Aphrodite?" He didn't shout her name, but rather it came out as a soft plea.

A woman in a dark-red evening gown appeared. He fell to his knees, clutching at her skirts.

"Take me back, please. Take me back to her." His eyes stung with tears. He would beg. He would grovel. He would do anything to be back with the woman he loved.

Aphrodite gave him a cold smile. "You have been granted all the mercy I am willing to give. I returned you to your time, at her request."

She asked that he be returned to his time and not to her? His heart seized. It couldn't be true. Surely she felt the same for him as he did for her.

"You have your life back—that is all that matters. You're free to return to your former life." Aphrodite waved her hand around the gardens and smiled. "We were in the midst of a celebration when this all began, don't you remember? And I feel you've learned your lesson, perhaps even enough to please me now as you should have before. Care to try again?" She stroked her fingertips down his cheek, an affection- ate, lust-filled gaze in her eyes.

Devon lowered his head. His heart sank toward the ground, as if to bury itself in the soil, never to beat again. He let go of her fine silk skirts and touched the ground, palms flat on the earth.

"I'm sorry, my goddess. But I cannot."

She reached down to lift his head to face hers again. "Such an offer is not lightly made. You dare risk angering me a second time?"

"I beg your forgiveness, but I cannot give you what you want, because my heart belongs to another.

I will love no one but her. If you cannot send me back, then I beg of you one final request."

The goddess said nothing, but she waited for him to continue.

"Please find it in your heart to send her a man who will care for her in all the ways I wish I could." His voice was hoarse, but he got the words out past the icy grief stealing through his soul.

Aphrodite's blue eyes widened. "Why?"

"She has lived a life without proper love, and I cannot bear to think of her going on without it. I want her to be happy, to be loved. It is my only wish." And he meant it from the depths of his soul and beyond.

Aphrodite leaned down and cupped his face in her hands. She kissed him softly, not as a lover but as a queen to her subject. "Then you truly have learned to put someone before yourself. In three days, I shall meet you here and ask you if you wish to return. Be certain of your decision, for I will never offer it again."

Three days...he could see his family, say his farewells, and go home to Rebecca.

"Yes, I accept."

"Very well." A small smile curved her lips.

He had but a moment to see a constellation of stars winking in her eyes before everything went dark.

IT HAD BEEN THREE WEEKS SINCE REBECCA HAD lost Devon. Three long weeks without dancing, without laughter, without love. But she'd rallied and forced herself to get out of bed each morning and go to work. She had to. She didn't know what else to do.

It seemed Aphrodite didn't like to leave loose ends. A replacement statue had magically appeared the night before the big exhibit launch with her boss none the wiser. She'd gone into the gallery several times to see it, hoping against hope she'd find it missing again and instead have her living, breathing lover before her once more. But it never happened. The statue remained there on its pedestal, stoic and sightless...merely sand and stone.

She reminded herself that somewhere in the distant past Devon was living his life. *Had* lived his life. He was long gone, and all that remained were faint echoes of their time together. Evan sat on the couch, sighing heavily each night when she went to bed as though he missed the man who'd become a part of his life just the way Devon had become a part of hers.

After the first day of him being gone, she'd checked the ancestry site, and when she hadn't seen him appear on his tree, she'd been worried. Perhaps he'd never married and didn't show up as a possible connection to later descendants. She'd found his death date as September 1816, but she hadn't been able to stomach the thought that he really had died then. Surely Aphrodite wouldn't have let that happen. If she had...Rebecca's stomach churned again. Would she ever know Devon's fate?

Rebecca came home from work, her feet aching from wearing heels again, but she'd stood up to her boss today and told him that his dress code requirements were not only uncomfortable, but unfair—this was the twenty-first century, dammit. She'd also said in no uncertain terms that his OCD issues were counterproductive to the smooth operation of the museum and that if he kept it up, she was going to quit.

He'd actually backed off. She couldn't believe it. She'd figured out how to handle him and had finally been given more freedom with the exhibits and her responsibilities—not to mention free drinks for life from her female coworkers.

She unlocked her front door and kicked off her shoes, happy to see Evan prancing excitedly by the front door. He clearly needed to be let out.

"Hey, big guy." She ruffled his fur and kissed his head. She buried her nose in his coat, inhaling the scent, surprised that he smelled like the outdoors. A

Wheaton Terrier's fur often carried the aromas of whatever they'd been nearest. She breathed in the scent of trees and fresh mown grass, puzzled. He hadn't been outside in hours. Mystified, she released Evan and he nuzzled his mouth against her hands and face before he sat back on his haunches and barked at her twice.

His tongue lolled from the side of his mouth, and he started bouncing toward the living room. That was when she smelled the most divine aroma. Had she left something in the oven when she'd come home for lunch? Worried, she rushed into the kitchen and froze when she saw a man bending down over the oven, lifting out a glass dish with baked chicken.

"Just in time." That familiar, wonderful accent was like the strains of a favorite melody she hadn't listened in ages.

"Devon..." She choked down a sob as he turned to face her, removing his oven mitts.

He opened his arms, and she flung herself into his embrace. "Rebecca."

This is a dream; maybe I died driving my car home from the museum. It can't be him, it can't be...

"Don't cry. I promised I would never let you cry again because of me. I would hate to be caught in a lie." His lips brushed her ear, and she blinked away the rush of tears and sniffled. She nuzzled against his chest, as though she'd been missing a piece of herself for so long and now she was...whole. She kissed him hard even as she tried to convince herself this was real, that she wasn't dreaming.

"She... Aphrodite said she wouldn't let you come back to me," Rebecca confessed between sniffles and kisses. "It was either the stone or sending you to back to your life in the past. I begged her to send you back home so you could live."

"I begged her to send you a man who would love you as I wished to. She said I had learned my lesson and sent me back to you."

"But why did she wait three weeks?"

He hesitated. "She gave me three days to say my farewells to my family and sort out my affairs, and I spent the last two and a half weeks seeking employment and settling in here. I've been living in Mrs. Lesley's spare bedroom."

Rebecca stared at him. This whole time when she'd been picking up the pieces of her heart and trying to get her life back together, he'd been next door?

She smacked him across the cheek and then immediately started to cry. He held her tight, whispering in her ear.

"I'm sorry. I wanted to come to you more than anything. But I felt I had to find employment and a decent wage before I could come back. You deserve a man who can provide for you and your home." When he said the word *home*, it rocked her to her core because it was true. This was his home.

And he's my home.

"I'm sorry, I just... Three weeks, Devon. My heart... I can't take that again."

"You'll never have to be without me again, I promise."

He lowered his head to hers, and their lips brushed in a melting fire of passion. The glowing pulse of love that sparked between them could never be extinguished. The will of an angry goddess had brought them together. Rebecca was never going to let Devon go. And by the way he looked at her with a twinkle in his eyes, he wasn't going to let go of her either.

He chuckled. "Who knew it would be such a blessing to be cursed?"

"Who indeed?" Rebecca laughed, but they both shivered when they heard that bell-like sound of a goddess's laughter ringing in the air all around them.

Who indeed...

Wait! Don't turn off that kindle! I have some awesome news to share with you super quick

plus a 4 chapter preview of a sexy dragon shifter romance you don't want to miss!

I give away 3 FREE romance novels! Fill out the form at the bottom of this link and you'll get an email from me with details to collect your free read! The free books are *Wicked Designs* (Historical romance), *Legally Charming* (contemporary romance) and *The Bite of Winter* (paranormal romance).

Claim your free books now at: http://laurensmithbooks.com/free-books-and-newsletter/

Here's were you can find me on social media!

My Main Website

Facebook

Instagram

Twitter

Private Facebook Fan Group

Wattpad

I share upcoming book news, snippets and cover reveals plus PRIZES on all of the above places!

NEVER MISS A NEW BOOK OR A DISCOUNTED BOOK! FOLLOW ME HERE FOR ALERTS:

Amazon
Bookbub

**Turn the page to read 4 chapters from *Grigori:
A Royal Dragon Romance* now!**

GRIGORI: A ROYAL DRAGON ROMANCE

CHAPTER 1

"*Here there be dragons.*"

—Note on a map from the Age of Exploration, regarding Terra Incognito.

Blue and silver scales whispered against grass as the giant beast crawled across the field toward Madelyn Haynes. Rain lashed her skin and lightning laced the skies. Smoke billowed from the beast's nostrils, and his amber eyes narrowed to dangerous slits as it crept closer. There was no escaping. The creature had finally found her and would destroy her. It had already killed tonight and would kill again. Ash infused the air, the scent of smoke choking her. Fear and rage filled her, drowning her with the overwhelming sensations until she was torn between two instincts: fight or flight. Her skin tingled, the feeling building until it felt like she was on fire.

A man was shouting . . . *"Run!"*

The beast turned away from her, searching for the person who'd cried out a warning but it was no use. The creature would kill her too once it found her.

There was no way she would survive. She was going to die . . .

"No!" The word was a silent scream upon her lips as she tried to run.

Boom!

Madelyn jolted upright, her mouth open in a strangled shout. The covers of her bed were wrapped around her legs, and she kicked out trying to free herself. Panting, she clutched her head as a dull throbbing ache beat behind her temples. She breathed in and out, focusing on each breath and the tranquility it gave her before the headache subsided and her heart stopped pounding against her ribs.

Then she turned on the light by the bed in her small hotel room and reached for her sketch pad and pencil. Using pillows to prop herself up she flicked to a fresh page and began to draw. The lines came easily, as they always did when she had the nightmares of the beast. It left such a vivid image in her mind that she had no trouble bringing it to life on the page. As the sketch began to develop, she knew what she would see. A serpentine creature with an elegant snout, two large wings and a long tail that could snap back and forth like a whip.

A dragon.

For as long as she could remember, whenever it rained, she dreamed of that same dragon. Rain, scales, lightning, and a crashing sonic boom that rattled her awake.

Madelyn studied tonight's dragon. It was blue and silver with a deep sapphire underbelly. The webbing of its wings was a fainter, almost icy blue. It had a large, almost lizard-like frill that fanned up around its head like a lion's mane which was that same glacial blue as its wings. It was an eerily beautiful creature with fierce eyes and sharp talons and was in a predatory crouch as though ready to hunt her down. Madelyn's hand trembled as she set the pencil down and stared at the dragon. A part of her had hoped that leaving the United States—and changing her surroundings—would make her feel less trapped, less hunted. But the nightmares had followed her.

She was still being hunted.

She'd come all the way to Russia to save her career. As a professor in medieval mythology, she had been reading and researching dragons for the last five years. But lately she'd become convinced, as insane as it sounded, that dragons might have been real at some point in history. She was hoping to prove that some remnants of dinosaurs had remained alive into the time of humans, and that could explain the unique collection of global mythology around dragons. How else could dragon myths around the world have such eerie similarities? Something told her there was a kernel of truth to each myth she'd come across, but she had to find a way to prove it.

Or else I'm fired.

Ellwood University had given her a three-month sabbatical to either pursue her theory and prove it, or drop it and attempt to tie her research to more traditional projects. Madelyn had collected her meager savings and rented this hotel room by the month in the Tverskaya district of Moscow.

Outside her window she could see the distance lights of the city and hear the low steady hum of traffic. Moscow was so different from her small town of Shelby, Michigan. Instead of a Russian concrete jungle and tangle of complex cityscapes and police sirens at night, the Midwestern air was filled with the hum of crickets and the throaty songs of frogs in the ponds. Some nights the breeze from Lake Michigan would slip through the windows and soothe her as she slept. Even the winters in Michigan felt pure, clean, not like the dark, dirty snow-covered streets of post-soviet Moscow.

With a shiver of longing for home, Madelyn set the sketchbook aside and glanced at the clock. It was

6 AM. There was little point in staying in bed for another hour. She had to visit the Russian State Library and a few small antiquarian bookstores which could take up most of the day. She'd been here one week and had settled into a routine. *Sleep. Research. Eat. Research. Home. Sleep.*

She had come to Moscow alone and was hesitant about going out on her own after dark. She spent most of her evenings cuddled up in the armchair by her bed, reading. It was certainly safer than going out. Madelyn needed to feel safe. She feared the unknown, and what might be around the corner.

A therapist had once diagnosed her airily with a generalized fear of the unknown, citing trauma from her parents' deaths. She had been two years old, too young to remember the details though she'd been with them when they'd died. Too young to know her own name or where she came from. Neither of her parents had IDs when the police found her in the wrecked car that had rolled into a ditch during a storm. Her name, "Madelyn", had come from the name stitched onto her baby blanket. Her adoptive parents, the Haynes's, had wanted her to keep that name.

Thoughts of her birth parents always made Madelyn sad and oddly helpless. She wished she could have done something to save them from the car crash. She knew that there was nothing a baby could have done, but it didn't erase the helplessness. For a long moment, Madelyn watched the rain outside and rubbed one hand absently on her chest where her heart ached. And then, she did what she'd always done. She buried the memories and the pain and turned her thoughts to her research. It was the best distraction. There was nothing like wandering through the stacks of a library and letting the musty scent of ancient books overwhelm her. It was one of the reasons she'd been drawn to history when she was in college. Surrounding herself with the past, she knew what had happened, and couldn't be shocked or surprised . . . was comforting.

Madelyn crawled out of bed and stripped out of her clothes before she jumped into the small shower, cringing as she expected the icy blast of the spray. There was only so much hot water before it turned cold she couldn't stand a cold shower in October in Russia.

Two hours later, she was dressed and had filled her backpack with notebooks and other research related materials. When she stepped out on the street in front of her hotel, her nose twitched as it picked up the harsh scents of the city. People bustled past her in a frenzied haste to reach their jobs, and for a strange moment Madelyn felt rooted in place as humanity flowed around her. An eerie sense of being watched made the tiny hairs on the back of her neck raise up.

Of course she was being watched. This city was home to millions of people; someone would always be looking at her no matter what. The uneasy sensation inside her didn't disappear, even when she hailed a cab and headed for the Russian State Library.

The State Library was a beautiful architectural cross between Soviet era design and classical design, which called back the days of the Czars. The smell of musty texts and recently cleaned marble steps were a welcome mix of aromas that always calmed Madelyn.

She walked up the white stairs to the upper decks of the library, her eyes dancing from the blue marble columns to the endless shelves.

17.5 million books were here . . . Her heart sped up at the sheer thought of having a world of infinite stories at her fingertips. But she wasn't here to see their vast array of novels. She was here for one book. A heavily guarded tome that required supervision whenever it was handled.

She kept walking and left the modern rooms behind before reaching a wing of the library that housed antiquarian collections. One of the collection areas was a beautiful two-story room with gleaming walnut bookcases illuminated by hanging golden globes of light. A slightly domed ceiling was painted with scenes of Greek mythology, the gods on Olympus displaying their power and might.

A security guard stood at the back of the room by

a small reception desk and he waved her over. He greeted her with a warm smile and spoke something in Russian which she thought sounded like hello. She was still listening to her Russian audiotapes and hadn't picked it up as quickly as she'd hoped.

"Good morning," she greeted back. He was different than the guard from yesterday.

"Ahh, English, I help you?" he asked in with a heavy Russian accent.

Madelyn smiled. She'd been relieved to discover that many of the guards were fluent in English to a degree. She knew enough of modern Russian to get by but her specialty was the rare dialect East Old Slavic which she used to read older Russian primary resources.

"I'd like to check this book out please." She retrieved a small piece of paper with the name of the edition in English and Russian and its location on the shelves. The guard read the card and then his brown eyes looked from it to her face, studying her.

"This volume? You are sure?" he asked, his voice was oddly hushed and his face drained of color. He stroked his security badge on his chest with one finger as though he'd done it a thousand times when nervous. He glanced around the room, which was almost entirely empty save for another researcher, an elderly man, who was buried in a stack of what looked to be medieval texts. The man glanced up at them, squinted, and pushed his glasses up his nose before returning to his work. The guard stared at the man for a long moment before he turned his focus back to Madelyn.

"Please, miss, I could get many other books for you, but this one . . . Are you sure?" It was the second time he'd asked that question, and it made her skin prickle.

"Yes. That one." Madelyn assured him. Why was he so protective of this one? This entire room was filled with ancient texts that with proper care could be viewed by researchers. The guard sighed slowly, his face turning red as he nodded to himself and muttered in Russian.

Now she was feeling really anxious. She'd checked out several tomes yesterday but hadn't discovered this particular text until she was pouring over the ancient collection of card catalogues that looked as though they'd been written half a century before. There on the yellowed paper of the cards, in ink that was turning brown, she'd read the name of the volume *My Year With Dragons*. The library had been about to close and she only had time to scribble down the book's information before a guard politely escorted her out of antiquarian collection area. Surely today this guard would let her check it out . . . it was just a book after all.

The guard stared at the card again and then

nodded. "*Dah*, okay, we get you this one. Sit, please." He pointed to a small research table near one of the vast glass windows. Then he took a card and walked over to the shelves on the opposite side of the room.

While he retrieved the book, Madelyn set out her notebook and pens with shaking hands before she donned a pair of library approved white gloves to handle the books safely. Why was the guard so hesitant to give it to her? From the text's description in the card catalogue that she'd be able to translate, it was a memoir of an English man who had spent time in Russia. There was no political or social discourse in it that could prompt a Russian security officer to be concerned . . . But he had been. The man had looked ill at the thought of fetching that tome.

She peeped at the guard from the corner of her eye. He unlocked a glass case on one of the shelves, his head cocked to the side as he squinted at the titles on the spines. Then he used his index finger to gently tug a shorter leather-bound edition free of the case. Once he had it in his hands, he didn't immediately come over to her. For several seconds he stood there, holding the book and staring at her. His lips were pressed tight in a grimace as he finally walked over to her.

"Please be careful. This is special book." He held out the leather bound tome and Madelyn accepted it. Her skin tingled again as she felt the smooth leather in her palms but she hid her reaction. The guard nodded at her again and then walked back to his station.

Madelyn's skin continued to tingle as she lifted the leather tome to get a closer look. The cover was made of thick leather, bare of any titles or identifying marks except the initials *J.B.* in the bottom right corner. Madelyn smoothed her fingertips over the initials and opened the front cover. The title was written on the front page in pen and ink. Not in typeface.

My Year With Dragons—A personal collection of observations about my time spent with the Barinov family, by James Barrow. Dated 1821.

Madelyn whispered the words. It was written in English, and James Barrow could be English or American. She held the text in one hand and made a note in her notebook before she turned to the next page.

Her heart stuttered to a stop in her chest.

Three pencil sketches depicted the faces of three different men. Names were scrawled beneath each intimate portrait.

Mikhail, Rurik and Grigori. The Barinov Brothers.

The first man, Mikhail, seemed more brooding, his hair dark and his eyes almost black. He seemed worried, but he was attractive and even the shadows that haunted his eyes were enchanting. In the second drawing, the man named Rurik had dark hair and mischievous eyes, with a playful, charming grin on his lips that outshone the white scar drawn from above his right eyebrow down to his cheek as though he'd been slashed. He looked like a bit of a troublemaker but the thought made her smile.

Her eyes lingered longest over the sketch of the man named Grigori. Something about him stilled her, like the moment she stood outside on the first snowfall of winter. There was a strange whispering at the back of her mind, a collection of hushed voices that she couldn't seem to hear clearly enough to understand. She was fascinated by the man's handsome face, the pale hair and light eyes. There was a melancholy beauty to his lips, and an almost rueful smile barely hinted in the drawing—as though he had sat still long enough to assist the artist but as soon as he was able, he'd move again.

While all three men were intriguing, it was Grigori that Madelyn's eyes came back to over and over. Something about his face . . . Like a half-remembered dream. Deep inside her, there was a stirring, as though a part of her she never knew existed had awoken. The voices didn't stop that whispering and Madelyn couldn't help but wonder if she was going mad. Between the dreams at night and now this . . . She drew a deep breath in and let it out, slow and measured, calming herself.

Stay focused on the research.

"Grigori," she test his name upon her lips, finding she liked the way it sounded, the syllables strong and yet soft.

She wanted this sketch. The compulsion to possess his likeness was too strong. She glanced about the room and saw the guard was on his phone, texting and not looking her way. Sneaking her cell phone out, she flicked on the camera and snapped a hasty picture of each of the brothers before she put it back in her purse. Hands trembling, she turned the page again, forcing herself to look totally calm and not like she'd been taking photographs of a protected manuscript.

The next page was a diary entry dated March 16, 1821.

"Dragons are real . . ." The first words of the entry made her body shiver and a sudden chill shot down her spine. She forced herself to keep reading and couldn't help but wonder what James Barrow meant. Dragons weren't real, at least not in the fire and brimstone sense. She was convinced that some extinct reptile species were behind the legends, but there was no such thing as *real* dragons.

"I met the Barinov brothers in Moscow and learned they were not mortal men . . . they were possessed of strange abilities. The touch of fire, the breath of smoke, the eyes that glowed . . ."

What the hell? Madelyn reread the last few

sentences. What was Barrow saying? She'd expected the volume to recount tales of large serpents or lizards that Barrow must have encountered on his journey. As a naturalist, he would have been out in the field exploring different species of animals, and he could have easily glimpsed an ancient breed of reptile that looked dragon-like. The Komodo dragon was a modern example of what many rural cultures still believed were the descendants of dragons. It was part of her theory for her research. But Barrow wasn't talking about Komodos or any other type of reptile. He was discussing men . . . Men who had powers. Perhaps the word dragon was simply a metaphor Barrow was using?

She glanced down the page and saw a smaller drawing of a man's hand and what looked like an elaborate ring. When Madelyn peered at it more closely, she recognized the style. The metal of the ring had been formed into the shape of a serpent biting its own tail, the symbol for eternity or the cycle of renewal. An *ouroboros*. Another dragon connection, but still not the type of dragon she was searching for.

Rather than read the rest of the journal entry, she turned the next several pages and paused when she came across a full page sketch. The drawing of a sleek, serpentine beast perched on a rock outcropping overlooking the sea made her breath catch as much as Grigori's portrait had. The beast sat back on its haunches and its large wings were flared wide, the clawed tips arching outward as though it was ready to fly. A barb-tipped tail curled around its legs. It was both a beautiful beast and a creature of nightmares, with gleaming teeth ready to snap. Reptilian slitted eyes stared straight ahead at her. The beast in her dreams came rushing back, the hiss of smoke escaping the nostrils, the puffs of breath as he prepared to spew fire, the lashing tail . . .

Beneath the sketch was one word. *"Grigori."*

But the sketch was of a man, not a dragon . . . Was this one of the men with supposed powers?

Whatever this journal was, it was clearly the workings of a man prone to flights of fancy and not a real naturalist. Disappointment made her heart drop to her feet and her shoulders slump. She'd been so hopeful to find a book that could show an anthropological connection to the dinosaurs or explain the worldwide dragon mythology. But this journal was not the answer.

Even though she wanted to keep reading, it wasn't a good idea. Many a good scholar who lost their way down a strange research rabbit hole had to find their way back to good solid research. She refused to let this one odd little book stump her. Better to put it back and move on. Still . . . she wanted just a few more photographs of the book; it couldn't hurt to read it over as long as she didn't use it for her research.

She surreptitiously took pictures of the next twenty pages before she hid her cellphone back in her backpack. Closing the book, she started at the leather surface, wishing she didn't have to give it back. Indecision flitted through her, but there was no real choice. It wasn't hers, and she couldn't keep it. With a sigh, she rose from her research table and walked back over to the security station and held the book out the guard.

"Finished?" he asked, his eyes fixing on the book rather than her as though he was anxious to snatch it out of her hands.

"Yes, it wasn't what I was looking for." She almost didn't let go when he tried to pull the book away from her. Finally the leather journal slipped through her fingers.

"Thank you," she said to the guard. With a heavy heart, she returned to her study station and collected her notebooks and papers before removing her gloves and tucking them back in her bag. Each step away from Barrow's mysterious journal left her feeling cold and distanced in a way that made little sense. A soft feminine voice, like the hum of a murmur from a dream teased her mind.

He has the answers but you're too afraid to see . . .

Madelyn shook off the thought. The notes in

Barrow's journal were impossible to believe. He clearly didn't know what he was talking about. He was rambling on about men with powerful abilities and drawing beasts more suited to a role-playing fantasy computer game than he was about creatures that tied to real mythology.

She would have to start back at the catalog again, but she had no energy to hunch over the little metal filing cabinets squinting at poorly scribbled titles and book descriptions the rest of the day.

Maybe I could take a day off. Wander around the library a bit and explore.

The architecture was beautiful and she hadn't really had a chance to examine it before. As she exited the antiquarian room she glanced back one last time. The security guard was holding the journal, and he was speaking into his cell phone. He was also staring right at *her*.

That sense of being watched and being talked about was too strong this time to ignore. The guard said something into the phone and rather than put the book back on its shelf, he set it down and put a hand on his gun holster at his hip.

"Miss, please come back," he said, taking a meaningful step in her direction. "My superior wishes to speak to you. You cannot leave."

"He does? Why?" she asked, her muscles tensing and her hands tightening on her bag.

"The book you chose, he has questions . . ." The guard said, his gaze darting around her as though expecting someone to come and help him. "Sit down, now." His tone was more forceful than before.

Madelyn knew she should stay put, talk to him . . . but her instincts suddenly roared to life and the only thought that flashed through her head was *run . . . run fast*. Body shaking, she stumbled on trembling legs to flee.

She shoved open the door and sprinted down the hall, hitting the top of the long set of stairs at a brisk run. Everything around her seemed to blur, and her heart was pounding hard enough to explode from her chest. Covering the steps in seconds, she forced herself to slow when she realized people were staring at her. That was the last thing she needed, people seeing a panicked woman fleeing a Russian library like a crazy person. It was a conspiracy theory in the making.

Her breath was labored and her body was shaking with a surge of adrenaline as she tried to walk calmly out of the library. The crowded streets were a blessing as she melted into the flow of people. She only looked back once and caught a glimpse of the security guard from the collections room. He stood at the top of the Russian State Library steps, his gaze scanning the crowd. He was still on his cell phone, talking rapidly.

Lowering herself by hunching over, Madelyn slipped down a side street to catch her breath. What the hell just happened? Sure, she'd snuck a few pictures of a text, but why would he chase her? She hadn't seen any rules about no photography in that section of the library. Why had the guard chased her?

What about James Barrow's book was so dangerous that men would look for her?

Grigori's face and the body of the fierce dragon like beast flashed across her mind. *What have I stumbled onto?*

CHAPTER 2

"Peace, Kent! Come not between the dragon and his wrath."

—William Shakespeare, *The Tragedy of King Lear*

Grigori Barinov stood in front of the floor-to-ceiling windows in his executive office, staring out over the city of Moscow. Body alert, every muscle rigid, the expensive gray wool suit he wore felt tight as he shifted. Below him, people were passing on the streets. A flash of silver caught his attention. It was the wink of a diamond earring dangling from a well-dressed woman's ear. With eyes that were ten times as powerful as a mortal's, he scanned the streets, absorbing every detail.

Searching . . .

For the last few days, his senses had picked up on something in his city. A creature he didn't recognize. It made him restless. Moscow was filled with supernatural beings—werewolves, vampires, shifters of all kinds, and magically gifted humans were all present—but none of them fired up his instincts. No, he'd never felt this before in his life, but he knew in his gut what it was. An enemy was in his city, a creature that posed a threat to him. As a dragonshifter, few creatures in this world could give him pause and put him on his guard. He only wished he knew what sort of beast it was so he could hunt it down and remove the threat.

The sapphire dragon tattoo on his forearm itched, but he didn't scratch it. He knew the dragon inside of him was trying to warn him to stay on his guard. The phone on his desk buzzed and his personal assistant, Alexis spoke.

"Mr. Barinov, you have a call from the Russian State Library."

Every muscle in his body tensed. There was only one reason anyone from the Russian State Library would be calling him. That damn book by James Barrow. He'd been too softhearted and Barrow had been so earnest. He'd gone against his better judgment and allowed the Englishman to spend a year studying him and his brothers. And he'd been paying for it for the last 200 years. He'd been lucky Barrow's heirs had sent him the journal. Thankfully, it had never been sent to a publisher; Barrow had kept his word about his writings remaining a secret.

I should've burned it. But he hadn't been able to. Barrow had become a friend and Grigori hadn't wanted to destroy the memory. There was also something fascinating about reading an insightful human's observations about him and his brothers.

He couldn't leave it at his office or his home in the country. His enemies had frequently broken into both places more than once, searching for anything they could use against him. He'd thought he'd be clever and tuck it away in a library amid other obscure texts that no one ever looked at in a guarded collection. It had been safe all these years, hiding in plain sight. Until now.

"Mr. Barinov?" Alexis queried again.

"Put the call through." He turned away from the window and walked over to his mahogany desk just as the phone rang.

He answered. "Yes?"

"Mr. Barinov, my name is Yuri. I'm a guard for antiquarian book room at the Russian State Library." A man spoke, his voice hushed and anxious.

"Yes." Grigori waited, his patience on a razor's edge.

"When I first took over security for this room I was given strict and confidential instructions to call you if anyone ever came asking about a certain title in the collection. Someone checked out the *Barrow* book, Mr. Barinov."

Grigori closed his eyes, holding his breath for a moment. "And?"

"I followed protocol. She did not leave the library with the book. But . . ." The guard hesitated. "She was taking pictures. I have no instructions regarding pictures." The phone cracked as Grigori's temper flared.

"Pictures?"

"Yes. She was using her phone." The guard's voice wavered as though he sensed Grigori's building rage.

Pictures. Fuck, if any evidence of his existence was discovered and exposed in the world of mortals it would put a target on his back and that of his two brothers. The magical world knew of his family, the last three brothers in ancient bloodline of Russian Imperial Dragon shifters, but the rest of the world didn't know . . . *Couldn't know*.

"Can you detain her until I arrive?" he asked the guard.

"But she's leaving now—"

"Stop her!" Grigori barked. The other end of the phone was full of panting, the flapping of rubber soled shoes on marble, a muffled shout for someone to stop. Grigori tried to picture the library in his mind, wondering why the guard couldn't catch up with this woman. Finally the footsteps stopped, and Grigori heard the sounds of streets of the city muted beneath the guard's gasping for breath.

"She ran—I couldn't catch her before she left the library. She's gone. But I have the book."

Grigori sighed. "I will come to collect it. When I do, I want every detail you have about this woman. Her name, where she's from, *everything*."

"Yes, Mr. Barinov," the guard replied, still breathless.

Grigori slammed the phone down and cursed. His hand was white-hot from his temper and he'd left burn marks on his expensive new phone. With a growl, he pressed the intercom button

"Alexis, please have someone replace my phone in the office. This one met with an unfortunate accident."

A second later his receptionist opened the door, leaning against it to look at him in concern. His dragon perked up beneath his skin at the sight of the woman's killer legs. She was staring at him, the perpetually hungry look in her eyes always an open invitation to share her bed, but he'd never once been tempted. Sure, he'd noticed, and his instincts, so close to the surface, never let him ignore a beautiful woman. But things had changed over the last hundred years. His skin didn't prickle with awareness

LAUREN SMITH

and excitement. His dragon didn't growl with arousal the way it had in his youth.

No one had truly tempted him enough in a long time to let his bestial urges run free. Had he been in a better mood a smile would have curved his lips. As a younger dragon, he would have bedded several succulent mortals in a day, breaking bed frames as he gripped the wood to keep from harming the females while he fucked them into oblivion. Now his bed was empty of companions, but he wouldn't sleep with just any woman. Not anymore.

"Another accident Mr. Barinov?" Alexis purred as she approached his desk.

"Yes, please order me a replacement."

"Of course." She held out a hand and he handed over the destroyed phone.

Her expensive perfume rolled off her in thick waves. The decayed floral aromas made his nose twitch even as she walked out of his office and closed the door behind her. He never liked perfumes. A woman's natural scent was a heady thing and shouldn't be ruined with perfumes.

He could almost hear his younger brother, Rurik, teasing him. *As if you know anything about women anymore. You haven't had a woman in over a decade, brother...*

It was true. He found women less and less appealing these last few centuries. His urge to mate, to find the one female in the world that was truly his, had started to drive him mad with frustration. When a dragon reached a certain age, they stopped running wild and craved the closeness of a long-term companion. Most dragons never found their true mates and settled to simply breed with other dragons for the sake of children and to cure loneliness.

His gaze dropped to a framed photo on his desk. It was one of the few of his parents in existence, from thirty years ago, just a few years before they died.

If I could be as lucky as them and find a true mate . . .

No mere woman would suit him. It had to be the right one, one chosen for him by destiny. He would know her by her addictive scent that would send his pulse racing and his blood pounding. If he kissed her, he would catch glimpses of her memories and she would see his. A bond would form the longer they spent together, making them inseparable.

I want that more than anything . . .

He was not going to be tempted by Alexis or any other woman. They would only pale in comparison to a woman who would truly belong to him. He wanted a woman of his own, one to share his heart and soul with. Despite being alive for almost three thousand years, he still hadn't found the one woman that was meant to be his.

The sad fact was he couldn't wait any longer. His

once great family, the Barinovs, had included almost a thousand dragons.

Now we are only three. We are a dying breed.

The loneliness he was facing was slowly killing him, an immortal creature. The idea was almost laughable but it was true. A longing for a true mate had haunted him to the point that he was dreaming about her and waking up in the dark, his arms aching for a woman who was never there. He might never find the woman destiny had made for him. It was time to settle, and find a dragoness who could bare him children and continue the line, even if it meant he'd never know true love and completion.

"Mr. Barinov, is there anything else I can do for you?" Alexis asked, her suggestive tone telling him in no uncertain terms that she was offering herself to him if he was interested, which again, he wasn't. She wasn't his type. He liked his women with soft curves, a little petite with sunny smiles and warm hearts. He hadn't met a woman like that in Russian in over a hundred years . . . He was tired of Alexis throwing herself at him when he continually turned her down.

"No." He almost growled the word. Frustration slithered beneath his skin making him irritable enough to snap at her.

Alexis blinked, her face pale as a sheet as she backed out of the room. Smart woman. Dragons tempers were nasty things and it was best to stay clear when a dragon was fuming.

He pulled out his cell phone and dialed one of the few numbers he called with any frequency.

"Grigori? What's up?" His younger brother answered, his voice half-laughing as though he'd been chuckling when he'd answered the phone. The thought made Grigori's temper deflate somewhat as affection for Rurik swelled in his chest.

"Rurik, we have a situation."

"What is it? The Drakor family again?" His brother's tone turned gruff and serious.

Grigori stroked his chin as he replied. "No. They are abiding by our current treaty and staying to the eastern half of Russia." It was true enough. The Drakors were notorious for their egos, and if they had been causing trouble in his territory, he would have heard about it.

Rurik blew out disappointed breath. "I miss the battles. What I wouldn't give for the Drakors to put one foot on our soil . . ."

"You battle dragons," Grigori was torn between groaning and laughing. "Always wanting to start a fight." He loved his little brother, but he was the first to jump without looking—which often put their family in tense situations when it came to matters of diplomacy with other dragons.

Rurik was the family warrior, the one best suited

for battle and to wage single combat against other dragons when territorial disputes arose. The Drakors were the other Russian Imperial breed of shifters that vied for dominance of Russia against his family. The Barinovs and Drakors had been enemies for centuries.

"So if it's not the Drakors, what's the matter?"

"Remember James Barrow?" Grigori turned back to his window once again, searching in vain for the creature he sensed but could not see.

"Of course. The Englishman who visited us in the Fire Hills. He was always drawing and scribbling away in that leather journal."

"Yes. A woman was taking pictures of his journal today at the Russian State Library."

"Fuck. That can't be good . . ."

"My thoughts exactly," Grigori affirmed. The journal was almost a handbook on dragons—their powers, their weaknesses—and it had dozens of pictures of the three of them specifically. They might as well have put a neon sign above his building saying *"Real Dragons Inside!"*

"Do you think she believes what he wrote down about us is true?"

"I have no idea, but no reason she has could be a good one. I'm going to the Library to collect the book now and learn everything I can about the woman who took the pictures. I want you to help me track her down."

"Meet me at the club once you have the book." Rurik hung up and Grigori slipped his phone back into the pocket of his trousers before he turned away from the window.

As he left his office, he ignored Alexis's hopeful wave and he took the elevator down to the first floor. Barinov Industries, the family company he created a hundred years ago, had withstood wars, famine, and the many regime changes of Russian governments over the years.

He was not going to let one woman with a cell phone camera destroy his empire. For the last eighty years especially, Grigori had suffered the charade of "retiring" every thirty years and leaving the company to his son, also named Grigori. He'd spend the next few decades pretending to age, dying his hair silver and having new passports and forged birth certificates. The intricate lies he laid in place to keep the company going had cost him time and energy. He would not let his work be ruined by some overly curious human female.

His car was pulled out in front with his driver ready to take him anywhere he wished.

"The Russian State Library," he ordered as he settled in the black leather seat of the sedan.

"Yes, Mr. Barinov." The driver pulled out in traffic and began to head towards the library.

Grigori barely looked at the passing scenery of Moscow, his entire being focused on this mystery woman. Why was she researching dragons, and how had she found out about Barrow's journal? She shouldn't have even been allowed to take it off the shelf. Grigori acquainted himself with the new library director and informed him that should anyone ask for the book he must be called immediately and they were not to check it out. The guard had clearly failed in his duties and Grigori would make sure the library director would have him fired.

The time had come to take Barrow's book home and destroy it once and for all. While he had fond memories of Barrow, the details and personal histories of him and his brothers must be protected and that meant burning the book to ash. And dealing with this woman.

The only mortals who knew of his existence, aside from the ones in service to his family, were supernatural hunters. Namely the international organization called the Brotherhood of the Blood Moon. Pesky creatures, hunters. They rarely came into dragon guarded territories; it was simply too dangerous. Maybe this woman was a hunter, or they had hired her to find and retrieve any info she could on his family. If that was the case, he had a very nice dungeon she could rot away in for the next fifty years.

"Here we are, Mr. Barinov."

Grigori climbed out and told the driver to wait for him. Then he quickly ascended the stairs and entered the library. The guard, Yuri, was waiting for him at the security desk.

"Mr. Barinov?" Yuri held out the faded leather bound journal and Grigori took it.

The leather was warm to the touch and he lifted it to his nose, inhaling. A lingering scent teased his nostrils, the feminine aroma inviting and enticing. For a long second Grigori simply drank in the rich smell . . . it was *pure*. The pheromone sweet, like ripe dragon fruit. He had not smelled something like that in some years. The woman was a *virgin* of child-bearing age.

Must have her . . . Need to find her.

His body went rigid as the scent continued to plague and torture his nose with irresistible sweetness. If there was one thing besides a true mate that a dragon couldn't deny himself, it was a virgin. A growl began to rumble at the back of his throat as he pictured himself finding this woman and curling his arms around her and breathing in her scent before he seduced her.

The old Grigori, the wild beast he thought had vanished this last century, was roaring back to life.

His dragon was pacing inside him, ready to be unleashed. He wanted to sink his teeth into this woman's neck and hold her still while he thrust into her over and over until she screamed with pleasure.

"Mr. Barinov?" Yuri interrupted the sudden lust and hunger in Grigori's thoughts.

"Who is she?" he demanded in a low growl.

Yuri swallowed hard and held out a photograph, a print of a security camera photo of a woman.

"She is American. Her name is Madelyn Haynes. She's a professor at an American university."

Grigori stared down at the colored photo. It was slightly blurry, but he could tell that the woman had long strawberry blond hair and soft features. An ordinary woman, yet there was something about her face that he found fascinating. The lush curve of her lips, a slightly upturned nose and eyes framed by dark lashes. He lived in a city where beauty was praised and often the only way to survive. This woman would not have been considered pretty by such standards, but Grigori liked her full curves and romantic features more than he did the harsh, bony runway models that populated the Russian nightclubs.

Yes, she would be quite a delight to lock away in his dungeon.

He turned away from the security booth and exited the library. Back inside his car, he texted Madelyn's information to his brother. Within a few minutes Rurik sent the address for a hotel near the Red Square. He texted Rurik to meet him at the woman's hotel. He had a plan to trap their cunning little virgin and he was not going to let her escape.

✦

ALEXIS PETROV SLIPPED INTO THE LADIES RESTROOM close to her office in Barinov Industries. Flipping the lock on the door so no one else could come in, she checked beneath the stalls to make sure she was alone. This was one of the few places she could make a call without being seen on surveillance videos. She dialed a number on the screen, hit call and waited, her heart pounding.

"Drakor here." The deep, growling voice sent shivers through her.

Dimitri Drakor was a veritable god, much like her own boss Grigori Barinov, but Drakor had promised her things Barinov never would.

Sex and power.

It had been too tempting to agree to spy on her boss the moment Drakor had taken her to his bed and promised her the world. All she had to do was tell him what Barinov was up to. It was her boss's fault—if only he hadn't ignored her! She was a former model and she knew she was gorgeous.

How can he ignore me? Me? I walked runways in

Milan and Moscow! Resentment prickled her beneath her skin and she scowled.

"Barinov just left his office. He received a call from the Russian State Library."

Drakor breathed softly on the other end of the line before replying.

"Do you know what he was going there for?"

Alexis flinched. "No. Only that the moment he hung up, he left. That means it's important, right?"

"Yes, perhaps," Drakor mused. "Call me immediately with any more news." Then the phone connection went dead.

Alexis stared at her reflection the mirror for a long moment, her eyes haunted and her face suddenly showing her age. All of the parties, the drugs, the nights with powerful men who never called the next day had been a waste. She was past her prime.

Desperation drives us all. She forced a false smile on her lips, unlocked the bathroom door and stepped outside. She needed to be ready for when Mr. Barinov returned.

CHAPTER 3

"I do not care what comes after; I have seen dragons on the wind of morning."

—Ursula K. Le Guin

No one followed me.

Madelyn sighed in relief as she peered around the corner of the next street and watched the tourists mingling by the entrance to the Red Square. After two hours of dodging through streets and ducking into shop doorways, trying to look too interested in cheap touristy knick-knacks, she was fairly certain the guard from the library hadn't come after her. Her heart was still beating hard, but the panicked quick breaths had slowed.

"You're fine, everything's fine," she whispered.

She smiled at an old man who pointed at some Lenin-shaped figurines, and she politely shook her head and walked away from his shop.

A young man selling food from a cart on the street caught her eye. She dug her travel wallet out and bought a bottle of water and a meat and cheese pie called a *pirozhki*. Her stomach grumbled as she took the pie and inhaled the tasty aroma. She'd been so focused on running she hadn't realized how hungry she was. As she ate, she kept her gaze alert for the guard, even though she was fairly certain he hadn't followed her. Even if he could find out her name from the library system, she hadn't had to supply any other information. The hotel would be a safe zone.

I hope . . .

Madelyn licked her fingertips as she finished the last bite of her *pirozhki*. She crumpled the wrapper of her pie and tossed it in trashcan before she sipped the last of her bottle of water. Then she followed the crowd across a busy street to her hotel. She was still a bit on edge, but if she got into her room, she'd feel more secure.

The hotel was a bit shabby on the outside, with a grey stoned façade. The faux glass windows of the lobby were slightly fogged with age, but she had a budget to live on and couldn't afford anything more expensive. She wasn't sure how long she'd need to stay in Moscow for her Russian dragon research. She would have been lying if she hadn't glanced at some of the more beautiful five star hotels when she'd been making her travel plans. They had taken her breath away with underground pools and fancy suites with endless amenities. It had been fun to dream about them, but she could never stay at a place like that, even for one night—no matter how incredible it would be to live like a princess in a king-sized bed and look out across the city from a deluxe room's balcony.

She pushed the doors to the lobby open and stepped inside. A faint tingling started beneath her skin, the fine hairs rising on her neck and arms in response. The air around her felt charged with energy, like the moment before a storm broke out. Madelyn paused, trying to assess the feeling inside her body as it responded to the sudden change in the air . . . A queer pulsing sensation began to build inside her, and a headache started to beat against her temples. She'd been fine just moments ago . . . Was her fear from earlier just now getting to her and her body was crashing from the adrenaline high she'd been on?

Maybe I just need to go take a quick nap in the room and take some Tylenol.

A man in blue jeans and a dark gray T-shirt was leaning against the wall by the elevators, his head down as he texted on his phone. Was he waiting for an elevator? He hadn't pressed the button . . .

Madelyn tried not to look directly at him, as some men viewed it as an invitation. Her backpack was still full with pamphlets her mother had sent her about how to travel safely in Russian alone.

She couldn't help noting his muscled arms and the general attractiveness of his body. When she joined him at the elevator, she glanced down at her shoes, staring at the scuffed black boots peeking out from her own jeans.

A little flush heated her cheeks as she realized how boring she must have looked. Not that she wanted this man's attention. She didn't, but she'd been all too aware in the last week how unremarkable she was. So many women here wore bright sexy clothes or sleek business suits. She didn't fit into either group with her jeans and a cream colored Cashmere sweater. Not to mention she was a bit on the curvy side and Russian women her age were rarely curvy. They all seemed to be rail thin and ready for the runways and catwalks.

The metal elevator doors swished apart. She and the man both entered the tiny metal cubicle and she hit the button for the fourth floor. He continued to text and didn't hit a button.

Maybe we are on the same floor?

The second the doors slid closed her headache got worse. It was like two invisible spikes were being driven into her temples. She leaned against the side of the door farthest from the man, struggling to breathe. It was as though something inside was trying to claw to the surface.

What is happening to me? Fear clouded her rational thoughts. *Am I sick?* Was there something in her water from the vendor? Had she been drugged?

The man lifted his head a few inches, the fall of his brown hair still shadowing most of his features from view. The door opened to her floor and she stared at him. Was this his floor too? He still hadn't pushed a button for a different floor.

Something was wrong. She swallowed and tried to stay calm.

"Excuse me," the man waved her to go. "Please, go first," he said. His voice low and soft with a musical accent.

"Thank you." She took two shaky steps into the corridor before she realized that something was off. He knew she spoke English? How—she turned around to see him getting out of the elevator behind her.

Oh God . . . was he following her? She'd been warned before going to Russia that human trafficking was a risk and she had to be careful. She struggled to find her key, cursing as she walked to her door and trying not to look too panicked. Shooting another glance behind her, she saw the man was walking the opposite way down the hall.

She exhaled and sighed in relief against the door just as her hands closed around her keys. But she was still shaking and her legs were unsteady. The invisible knot of tension inside her was thrumming hard now, and every fiber of her being was on edge. That old instinct to run was whispering at her.

The key stuck in the lock and she had to jiggle the keys two times before the deadbolt slide back and she was able to get inside. The apartment was dark. Hadn't she left the curtains open? *I know I did . . .*

The door clicked shut behind her and she set her backpack down on small desk. She took a moment to catch her breath, and let the last few seconds of fear subside. She was safe inside her hotel.

I just need to chill. Everything is fine.

Seconds later, the light next to her bed switched on. A man sat in the chair by her bedside table and lowered his hand from the lamp back to the arm rest.

Madelyn jumped, clutching her purse to her chest. Her throat worked but no sounds out. There was a man in her room. *Oh God . . .*

The light washed over his pale gold hair and the three-piece gray wool suit he wore. Her eyes tracked up his expensive shoes to the beautiful, masculine hands resting on the chair's arms. A thick gold ring wound around the little finger of the man's right hand. She squinted at it and then her heart leapt into her throat. The ring was molded into the shape of a serpent biting its own tail. It looked exactly like the ring in James Barrow's book . . .

"Ms. Haynes, we need to talk." The man spoke, his rich accented voice pouring over her like cognac.

She lifted her gaze to the man's face and her heart stopped beating.

It was him.

The man from Barrow's book.

Grigori Barinov. The melancholic look of an ancient king whose time of ruling had long since passed into the mists, like a Russian King Arthur. With blue eyes and blond hair, he was not what one expected of a Russian man. Most of the men she'd seen in Moscow had dark hair and dark eyes. Strength and virility rolled off him in waves with a dominant air of calm and control that came from years of mastering oneself. Something about that made her shiver deep inside.

"Who are you?" she whispered, her voice catching. Had she passed out in the elevator? Was she dreaming? There was no way this was happening.

He couldn't be Grigori Barinov. Grigori was a man who had lived and breathed and died over two hundred years ago. There was no way he could be sitting in her hotel room looking like an intimidating fantasy. She wasn't sure if it was a fantasy born of secret desires or a nightmare. He had broken into her hotel room whoever he was and that wasn't a good thing.

The man reached up to remove the leather bound book from his jacket. *Barrow's journal*.

"I believe you already know who I am." As he spoke his blue eyes seem to turn to yellow, then to red and then they glowed white hot.

"But . . . You . . . It's not . . ." She couldn't wrap her mind around what he was trying to tell her. It was insane. It wasn't possible.

"Possible?" His full, kissable lips curved into a slow cold smile that sent fresh shivers through her.

"How . . ." she struggled for words, picturing the massive dragon perched on the edge of a cliff by a sea.

Her skin was almost on fire now, the pain making her want to scream but she didn't dare move or speak.

"'How' is not a question I will answer, at least not here." He rose from the chair and she stumbled back a step. He was too tall, at least six foot four. So much taller than her own five foot five. His height made her feel too small, too vulnerable. He could easily overpower her if she couldn't find a way to get out of here . . .

His perfectly cut suit molded to his muscled form like a second skin and his throat above his collar was sun-kissed. How could he be even slightly tan in the middle of a Russian October?

"Look, I don't want any trouble." She backed up another step, glancing around. She needed to find her phone. It had some international minutes . . . but she had no clue how to call the Russian police. Never in life had she felt so foolish than she did in that moment. Why hadn't she learned how to contact the police? Would it even matter? A panicked despair battled with her determination to survive.

"We are past that, Ms. Haynes. You're a liability now."

A liability? "But I don't even know what was in that book that even matters—" She swallowed hard and took another step, praying she could get to the door, but then she'd have to beat him to the stairs, because the elevator was out of the question.

"Unfortunately *everything* in that book matters. You must come with me," he said, taking another step.

Madelyn tensed, her hand searching for the door-knob behind her. When she found it, she wrapped her fingers around it and turned. The door opened with her body weight against it. Rather than fall into the open hallway, she bumped into something warm and hard.

"Going somewhere, *malen'kiy tsvetok?*" someone said from behind her.

"Ahh!" She screeched but the man behind her grabbed her around the waist with one arm and covered her mouth with his other hand.

"Little flower?" Grigori asked the man behind her.

"She smells sweet," he replied gruffly.

Madelyn screamed against his hand but the sound was muffled. She kicked out her legs, knocking Grigori back a few steps. He clutched his chest and sucked in a breath, then lifted his head, scowling at her. She thrashed in the second man's arms, but there was no getting free. Blood roared in her ears. Grigori's eyes were blazing and he licked his lips before he spoke to the man behind her.

"Do you have her or not?" Grigori growled.

The man holding her tightened his grip and dragged her away from Grigori. How could he be a man from the past?

Grigori's eyes were back to blue, a pure, unfaceted color that glowed like a lake reflecting the summer sky. Madelyn stared into the blue depths and her limbs became too heavy to move.

"That's it, little one, let go," Grigori breathed, never taking his eyes off her. The hand around her mouth disappeared and yet she didn't scream or cry out. She was lost in his mesmerizing gaze.

"Let your mind go . . ." Grigori's voice wrapped around her, and she suddenly was falling through space and time. As her eyes closed she saw a distant horizon, a memory so old she never knew she had it . . .

The grass was as soft as velvet as she toddled over toward her parents. They were sitting beneath a tall redwood tree. Her father had his back to the tree with his legs spread so her mother could lay back against him in the cradle of his body.

"She's growing so fast," her father said, smiling, but a tinge of sadness colored his gray eyes.

"Not too fast." Her mother held out her arms to Madelyn. "Madelyn, come here."

Her legs wobbled as she walked over the spongy grass. When she reached her mother, the feeling of being warm and safe made her sigh and nuzzle her face in the crook of her mother's neck. Her father circled his arms around them both, holding them in an unbreakable trinity.

"Why can't we stay here?" her mother asked wistfully.

"It's too dangerous. We must keep moving."

Madelyn didn't fully understand the words, not as a child. She'd only known that they'd meant leaving the sunny fields and ancient redwoods.

"I wish she didn't have to grow up on the run like us." Her mother's voice was soft with quiet grief.

"I know, honey, I know. Maybe someday she won't live in fear as we do."

The memory started to fade and Madelyn sank deeper and deeper into a dreamless sleep, Grigori's face following her into the depths.

"Give her to me." Grigori held out his arms and his brother handed him the unconscious woman. The feel of her completely in his control, made him relax as they left the hotel room. From the moment he'd picked up her scent on Barrow's book earlier that afternoon, he'd been possessed of a wild need to find her. It hadn't helped that once they found her, his brother had been the one to grab and hold onto her. His dragon had hissed softly inside his head.

"How was she able to stay awake for so long?" Rurik asked. "You used to be able to knock out mortals in mere seconds. That took nearly two minutes." He stroked his chin thoughtfully as he eyed the woman in Grigori's arms.

The uneasy thought struck him too. A dragon shifter's gaze could mesmerize and short-circuit a human's mind and knock them out. But the little American woman had simply looked dazed at first. It had taken too long to affect her.

"Something isn't right about her," Rurik muttered as they entered the elevator and rode it down to the lobby. "She makes my skin crawl whenever I get too close. But she smells divine and I just keep thinking about how much I want to take her to my bed . . ." He leaned over and inhaled her scent deeply.

Grigori almost growled at his brother. This was

his woman, and he had no intention of sharing her. Rurik was a charmer who never slept with the same woman twice. He had no right to bed this singular beauty and move on.

"What you're smelling is her purity."

"Her what?" Rurik crossed his arms, scowling in open confusion.

It was easy to forget sometimes his younger brother was so young compared to him. There were things Rurik didn't know about their other halves, the dragons within.

"She's a virgin. You've probably never been around one of childbearing age. They put off the most enticing sent. It's irresistible . . . to some." He didn't want his brother to know just how intoxicating the scent was to him. Just a hint of it clinging to Barrow's book had captivated him. Now that he held the female in his arms, her aroma enveloping him completely, he was addicted to it.

"A virgin?" Rurik practically choked on the word.

Before either of them could speak, the elevator doors chimed and slid open. They walked through the empty lobby and headed for the sleek black sedan parked outside. Rurik and the driver helped him get Madelyn inside. Only a few people in the streets dared to stare as they left. Most humans knew when to avert their gazes when in the presence of dragons. Some instincts were still strong in them, and they sensed that Grigori and Rurik were not to be trifled with.

The entire ride to Grigori's apartment building he held Madelyn his lap, overcome by a possessive urge to never let her go. She was like a jewel, precious piece of gold that he wanted to secure in a safe haven and guard, even sleeping with one eye open. He smiled as he drank in the sight of her face. She was even lovelier than he'd expected. The glimpse from the security camera photo hadn't done her justice.

"Why are you smiling?" Rurik demanded suspiciously. "You *never* smile."

Despite his frustration with his brother, Grigori didn't stop smiling. "I don't know, I can't seem to stop it. But she's mine. Do you understand? You're not to touch her. Are we clear?"

Rurik's brown eyes blazed to life. "Is that a challenge?" If he had been in his dragon form, the ruffled frill about his neck would have stood up in an opposing way to make him look bigger, fiercer. As a battle dragon, it would have been a deadly warning to anyone save close family.

"It's not a challenge." Grigori returned the warning with a growl of his own. "She is mine, end of discussion. You have an entire city of women who worship you. You do not need this one."

Rurik huffed, the sound so similar to the disgruntled noise as he made in dragon form that Grigori laughed softly.

"It's not as though I know what to do with a virgin anyway," his brother muttered.

Grigori's smile only widened. Rurik may not know what to do with a virgin, but Grigori definitely did. It had been so long since he had the pleasure of making love to a woman and introducing her to the sensual world that awaited her, but it wasn't something a man forgot.

In that moment, he decided it didn't matter what Madelyn's plans were in regard to James Barrow's book. He would discover that soon enough, but he was going to seduce her and possess her. While he had the strength to force her, he'd never done that to any female. Any man could take a woman's body, but only a master could make them surrender to passion of their own free will. And he wanted Madelyn to surrender to him.

When they arrived at his penthouse, Grigori carried Madelyn to his bedroom and set Barrow's journal on the night stand beside the bed. She was still unconscious and would be for several hours. It would give him time to make arrangements. He was going to take her home, to his house in the country. It was a place he could be himself and not worry about the city or the restraints it placed on his dragon half.

Grigori removed Madelyn's coat and slipped her boots off before he placed a pillow beneath her head. Her hair was soft, like silk beneath his hands as he brushed it away from her face. Even just an innocent touch made his body tense with hunger. He had to regain control.

He retrieved a white mink fur blanket and draped it over Madelyn's sleeping form. Impulsively, he leaned over to brush his lips on hers before he turned off the lights and closed the bedroom door.

"You're acting very strange, brother," Rurik noted. He was leaning back the doorway to the bedroom.

Grigori bristled. "I am not acting any differently." He used the tone that Rurik would recognize as a warning to drop the subject. But Grigori knew he was acting differently. The little human was bringing out old instincts in him, ones he thought he'd mastered long ago.

As the eldest of their family, his duty was the preservation of their lands and its protection. It was also his duty to carry on their line by either finding his true mate or by breeding with an eligible dragoness. He couldn't afford to let himself become entangled with a mortal that would leave him open and vulnerable. The pressure of his duties had left him cool, aloof, and in many ways unchanged over the years. But he was willing to let that part of himself go in order to seduce Madelyn.

"Come into the kitchen with me," Grigori closed the bedroom door and they headed into his kitchen.

His brother trailed a fingertip along the onyx granite countertop. "You aren't considering starting a relationship with a mortal. You know that doesn't end well, at least not unless you promise to keep it to only one night. Let's not forget she was researching the Barrow journal, and the last time I checked, that made her a possible enemy. She could be working for the Brotherhood of the Blood Moon. Or worse . . ." His brother frowned. "She could be working for the Drakors. Better be careful with this one, Grigori. After losing Mikhail, we cannot take any chances."

"I know," Grigori replied, not admitting he was planning more than one night with Madelyn. The last thing he needed was his little brother lecturing him on relationships and not sleeping with the enemy.

Their middle brother, Mikhail . . . The mere thought of his name struck Grigori like a dagger to his heart. His brother was in exile. They didn't know if he was even still alive. The last time he'd seen Mikhail had been two hundred years ago, the year he had returned home and brought James Barrow with him.

We were the fools who spilled our secrets. Barrow had never intended his diary to be their potential downfall, but over the years it simply became a font of knowledge that no one expected to survive the ravages of time.

"Grigori, I know you. You hide in your office, running the family business and playing the part of a mortal, but you are not. You are the eldest Barinov dragon. You cannot lose yourself to some human female. Even assuming she's not helping to bring us down and destroy our family, she will make you soft and when she's gone . . . It will weaken you. You're acting like she's a possible true mate. Father warned us about mortals," Rurik said.

The mention of their father brought back ancient memories. It was strange to think that their father had only died only two decades ago. It felt as though he'd been gone for a lifetime.

"I remember." He shut his eyes for a brief moment and almost saw his father's face, the stern but loving countenance as he told Grigori and his brothers the rules of dragons. *"Never mate a mortal. When dragons lose their mates, they grieve deeply and don't live much past the moment their mate dies."*

"She isn't my true mate, it's simply her scent that's caught me. But I do plan to seduce her."

Rurik chuckled. "Father said that about mother, you know. He only wanted to seduce her and thought he could resist her being his true mate. They ended up mated for three thousand years."

"But Mother was a Dragoness, not a mortal,"

Grigori reminded him. He walked over to his stainless steel wine fridge and retrieved a fifty-year-old bottle of Bordeaux and a glass. He reached for second one but his brother interrupted him.

"None for me. I have to head back. The club needs me. Call if the little mortal gives you any trouble."

"She won't." He listened to the sound of his brother's laughter, scowling until he heard the door to his penthouse close.

Then he poured himself a glass of wine, retrieved a book of German poetry by Rainer Maria Rilke, and sat in his favorite chair by the fire place in the center of the room. His fireplace was a circular stone structure two feet tall and was full of glass crystals with flames powered by gas. The sight was intoxicating, like diamonds on fire. Two of his *favorite* things. He tried to lose himself in the poetry and not think about Madelyn asleep in the other room. The scent of her filled his head and made his body throb with an almost violent need, but he kept control. *Barely . . .*

CHAPTER 4

"If you are the dreamer, I am what you dream.
But when you want to wake, I am your wish,
and I grow strong with all magnificence
and turn myself into a star's vast silence
above the strange and distant city, Time."

—Rainer Maria Rilke

Madelyn woke slowly, the memories of parents she didn't know and the life she never had a chance to live fading to intangible presences at the back of her mind until they were half-forgotten dreams. Her eyelids were heavy and her tongue felt like sandpaper. She blinked slowly as the leaden feel of her limbs dissipated and the fog in her head lightened. She sat up, a thick blanket of white fur dropping down to her waist.

Fur? She stared around at the master bedroom she was in.

"Oh my . . ." The tall four-poster bed was made of dark black wood, a midnight blue bedspread beneath her and a mountain of feather-soft pillows behind her. She caught her reflection in a large mirror on a dresser table. Her face was ashen and her lips pale as she sat in a mountain of expensive white furs. Her hair was in wild disarray. She threaded her fingers through the messy mane and took a few steadying breaths. Where was she? She struggled to remember anything before she'd woken up here.

The elevator, the man following her, and then Grigori . . . in her hotel room.

Oh my God. I've been kidnapped.

She curled her arms around her chest for several seconds, just trying to calm her panicked breathing. They had kidnapped her and brought her here. A thousand horrible scenarios ran through her head of what they might to do with her . . . human trafficking being the worst. The thought of it brought bile up to her throat and she swallowed, gagging.

Just calm down. Just calm down . . .

Her body froze, and her heart stopped for a painful second before it jolted back into a steady beat. She summoned the scholarly side of herself to analyze her surroundings again. She needed to figure out where she was and what they wanted from her. Then she could plan her escape. Beside her on the table, was a leather bound book she was all too familiar with. James's Barrow's journal.

Heart still pounding, she pushed the furs down and slid off the bed. Her sock-covered feet sank into a creamy white carpet. Madelyn grabbed the nearest bedpost, her fingers gripping the spindle carved wood as she walked around the king-size bed. She moved through the room and caught a teasing sense of something dark, pine and masculine. A scent she'd recognized when she'd been standing close to the man in the suit who'd looked just like Grigori from the journal. He couldn't be Grigori. She didn't know his name, so she might as well call him that until she figured out who he really was.

Grigori. He was everywhere in this room, from the elegant furnishings to the clothes hanging in the closet. Madelyn wasn't sure how she knew it was his room aside from the lingering scent, but it just felt like this was part of his world. She couldn't explain it. She'd never been in a man's bedroom before and it was exciting and scary.

Why had he brought her here? How had they knocked her out? And why did he want to know why she'd been interested in James Barrow's book? She had a thousand questions and no answers. The smart thing would be to find her shoes and coat and get out of here . . . no matter how intrigued she was with the mystery of Grigori Barinov.

She bent down and looked in the closet and under the bed for her boots but couldn't find them. She had a sneaking suspicion he had hidden them to keep her from escaping. She approached the beautifully carved bedroom door, gripping the antique glass doorknob. Would it be locked? Was she a prisoner? She turned the knob and it gave beneath the pressure.

The door opened and she entered a small corridor, passing a lavish master bathroom with a large tub and an oversized glass shower. *Whoa*. The next room she entered opened into a huge library and an office. Then the apartment gave way to a large living room with the kitchen at the back and a dining room. A roaring fire in a square pit in the center of the living room sparkled over crystal stones. A wing backed chair facing the fire creaked slightly and a masculine hand extended past the arm of the chair as it swirled a glass of wine.

Someone was sitting there . . .

Madelyn held her breath, listening to every sound from the antique grandfather clock in the hall ticking away to the sounds of the man in the chair turning the pages of his book. The hand holding the glass suddenly disappeared and the chair creaked again as the occupant stood and turned to face her.

It was Grigori. He looked too damn sexy, and intimidating, in that expensive suit. His light hair fell across his blue eyes and he gazed at her with an unreadable expression. Her heart was racing again, and blood roared in her ears as she watched him, afraid of what he might do.

"You're awake," he noted. He moved slowly, setting the wine glass on the table beside his chair.

"Why am I here?" She was careful to keep a safe distance between them. They were facing each other, like two animals measuring each other up before they decided to fight or not. She wouldn't hesitate to throw anything at him within her reach to escape.

"You're here because you checked out a book."

His cryptic reply made her bristle. The last thing she should be was argumentative, but she suddenly wanted to be brave in front of him.

"Is that against the law?" she asked, tilting her chin. She may have been scared out of her mind, but she was not going to let him see it.

Grigori's lips twitched. "No, but that book belongs to me."

She stiffened. "Then why did you leave it in a public library? You do understand that's how libraries work, right?" How she had the nerve to be snarky, she'd never know.

He placed one hand on the back of the leather

chair, his finger slowly tapping a pattern as though he was channeling all of his energy into the movement.

"A fiery creature," he murmured. "I like that." This was uttered so softly she thought she'd imagined it.

"So you have the book back, you can let me go. I *can* leave, can't I?" Her eyes darted around the room, seeking out the front door. She inwardly groaned when she realized the only way out was behind him. She'd have to get past brooding, sexy, and *scary* Grigori.

"No, I'm afraid you cannot leave. I have questions that require answers." He took two steps toward her. It took everything inside Madelyn not to retreat. She sensed that any sign of weakness would trigger his animal instincts. He was an aggressive predator who looked too intense to be in this lush apartment.

"Ask your questions and then let me go." She wanted to curl her arms around herself, but instead planted hands on her hips.

Grigori arched one eyebrow, calmly removed his coat and laid it on the back of the chair. His gray wool vest showed off his muscular chest and his tapered waist. She licked her lips, nervous and all too aware of him and in way she shouldn't be given that he had kidnapped her. The image of his face in the journal, the sketch dated 1821, haunted her. It couldn't be the same man. That was impossible. But the likeness . . .

"Who sent you after the book?" Grigori asked as he rolled up the sleeves of his crisp white shirt. It revealed muscular forearms, which were also sun-kissed. Her skin prickled and she tried to swallow the lump of fear in her throat.

"No—no one sent me. I came here on my own."

Grigori nodded to himself, smiling a little as he walked over to the kitchen and opened a cabinet.

"Would you care for some wine? It's a fine vintage." He held up a bottle and a glass.

"Did you seriously just offer me a drink? You've kidnapped me! For god knows what reason. You'd better let me leave right now or—"

"Or what?" Grigori was studying her through hooded eyes. "Ms. Haynes, I understand you are frightened, but I'm not planning on harming you. We're merely going to have a discussion. Once I have learned all that I need, you shall be free to go."

"You . . . you promise?" She had no reason to trust him if he did make such a promise, but part of her wanted to trust him. Part of her was still fixed on the man in the journal, the one she felt she knew somehow from dreams within dreams.

"I promise. I have no intention of hurting you. I merely needed a chance to speak to you privately. On my honor." He touched his freed hand to his chest with his fingers curled into a fist. The motion was archaic, like something a knight from the Middle Ages might do as he pledged himself to the lord of a castle.

Madelyn weighed her options—not that she really had any. If she was trapped here she wasn't going to make a fool of herself trying to escape until she had a real chance. She wasn't sure if she believed him, but part of her wanted to. She'd never felt so torn in her life. All logic and basic instincts were screaming to run away from the man who kidnapped her, but there was a deeper part of her, whispering to her to stay and trust. It was like she was staring at his picture in the library all over again and she couldn't look away, couldn't leave.

If I play along, it might help me buy some time to figure out a real plan of getting out of here.

Grigori waved the bottle in the air. "Well?"

"Sure. One glass," she finally replied. *God, please don't let me trusting him a little be a huge mistake.*

"Good." He walked over, setting a glass directly in front of her on the black granite countertop. They were only inches apart now. His body so tall and intimidating compared to hers. A nauseating pounding started in her head and her skin tingled like it had in the elevator with that other man.

She closed her eyes, steadying her suddenly shaky legs. How was it that this man could rattle her? Was it because he'd kidnapped her and she was freaking out . . . or was it something else? She'd been scared plenty of times, but it had never been like this. This felt . . . different. She didn't feel right, like her body was trying to change inside. It didn't make sense.

A hand, *his* hand brushed a lock of her hair back from her face, leaving a sizzling sensation behind wherever he touched her. As she opened her eyes, she saw him lean close to her and inhale deeply.

"Are you sniffing me?" she asked in a shaky whisper.

He exhaled slowly, his full lips suddenly in a firm line. "You smell good. Too good," he growled softly. His hand reached up again, but it stopped inches from her. And that was when she felt it. A faint breeze ruffled her hair, playing with the strands. Grigori stayed motionless, his eyes narrowed. And just like that, the unexplainable breeze vanished.

Madelyn held her breath, hoping he would move first. He finally stepped back.

"Did Damien MacQueen send you?" he asked as he turned and walked away from her, back to the fridge. The distance growing between them seemed like a vast chasm. It should have been a relief, but it wasn't.

I am going nuts. Seriously nuts.

He opened the door and stared at the contents before shutting it and frowning.

"Who is Damien MacQueen?" she asked. The name was one she didn't recognize. Grigori stared at her for a long moment as though discerning whether she spoke the truth.

"So the brotherhood didn't send you." He placed his palms on the counter, leaning forward slightly as he stared at her. The man had that intense gaze down to a T. She was frozen in place, unable to look away from him as he watched her. She tried to study him back, analyzing the way his jaw seemed to be cut from Italian marble and his straight nose gave him an air of distinction. He was gorgeous—for a kidnapper.

"You are a professor?" Grigori asked.

"Yes, at Ellwood University." She lifted her glass of wine and tried to take a sip. The wine was soft and dark on her tongue. A truly expensive wine without any bitter aftertaste. The floral bouquet hit her taste buds and finished with a hint of smoky wood.

"You like to research?" he asked.

Weirdly, it almost felt like she was on a date. These were like the usual questions: Who are you? What do you do for a living? Do you like it? But this wasn't a date. It was the farthest thing from it.

"I do . . ." she hesitated, trying to figure out what to do.

"And you enjoy history?" he asked as he sipped his wine, his blue eyes still fixed on her in a way that made her uncomfortable.

"Yes," she paused, trying to focus on answering him but also staying alert. "History is steady. You know it's always going to be the same, no matter how much you look back on it. I like the predictability."

"But you fear the future," he mused.

She bristled. "I don't fear the future, I just . . . I just don't trust things to happen the way I want them to sometimes." She'd expected her visit to Russia to be a safe one instead of getting kidnapped by someone like him.

"You have nothing to fear in your future," he promised again. "At least not from me." There it was, that solemnity in his gaze that almost seemed to beg her to trust him.

The hanging lamps in the kitchen illuminated Grigori's golden hair as it fell into his eyes again. Madelyn had the desire to brush those gold strands away from his face with her fingertips. And that was a crazy desire, because this man had kidnapped her and she shouldn't want to be touching him.

"God, I've got a bad case of Stockholm Syndrome," she muttered. She lifted her wine glass to her lips and took another sip.

"Look, I don't know any Damien and I have no idea what the brotherhood is. You have your book back so I see no reason for you to keep me here."

He ignored her as he pulled out his cell phone.

"Are you hungry? I believe I'll have dinner brought up."

"I'm not—" her stomach rumbled treacherously and he had to hear it because he smirked. He was smirking at her . . .

"Dinner, then we talk." He dialed a number and spoke in rapid Russian to the person on the other end of the line. She had thought it was a rough language before but listening to him speak it sounded musical.

I really need to take more Russian classes. Her two semesters of Russian in graduate school didn't help her understand a word of what he'd just said.

"Will you please tell me who you are?" she asked as he pocketed his phone in his trousers. He retrieved his own empty glass to refill it with some wine. He poured the burgundy liquid into the glass and she stared at it before looking at him again.

"My name is Grigori Barinov."

Madelyn bit her lip. He could not be *the Grigori* from James Barrow's book. He had to be a descendent of the other man, maybe a great-great-grandson.

"Okay . . ." she whispered. "So you're descended from the man in the book. The one in the sketch?" She thought again about man's face, the melancholy smile and the almost indulgent gentleness. That man was a mystery, just as this man was, but this Grigori's features were harder, colder. She still had a strange longing to meet the man in the sketch.

"No. I am not descended from the man in the sketch. I *am* that man."

Madelyn laughed. "That's funny." She had plenty of people make fun of her over the years for dragon research.

"I do not jest, Ms. Haynes. You have stumbled into *terra incognita*. Do you know what that means?"

Madelyn swallowed thickly. "It means 'territory unknown.' I've seen it on old maps."

"Very good," Grigori praised.

He lifted his wine to his lips and took a slow sip, those blue eyes of his piercing her, pinning her in place. "And do you know what else those maps said exactly?" The clink of his glass on the counter was the only sound in the room because neither of them dared to breathe.

And then she said the words, the ones that had been stirring like a serpent in a dark cave at the back of her mind since the moment she brushed her fingertips over the sketch of his face in the book. Surely he couldn't be suggesting what she'd always been too afraid to even contemplate . . . The words hovered on the tip of her tongue as she stared at him, hypnotized.

"Here there be dragons," she whispered.

The words drifted between them and although she and Grigori stood six feet apart, that space ceased to exist. His eyes were no longer blue, but a molten gold color, the pupils sliding into reptilian slits. That was impossible . . .

"Here there be dragons," he echoed in a husky whisper, and Madelyn screamed.

CAN'T WAIT TO KNOW WHAT HAPPENS NEXT? Grab your copy Here!

OTHER TITLES BY LAUREN
SMITH

Historical

The League of Rogues Series

Wicked Designs

His Wicked Seduction

Her Wicked Proposal

Wicked Rivals

Her Wicked Longing

His Wicked Embrace (coming soon)

The Earl of Pembroke (coming soon)

His Wicked Secret (coming soon)

The Seduction Series

The Duelist's Seduction

The Rakehell's Seduction

The Rogue's Seduction (coming soon)

Standalone Stories

Tempted by A Rogue
Sins and Scandals
An Earl By Any Other Name
A Gentleman Never Surrenders
A Scottish Lord for Christmas

Contemporary
The Surrender Series
The Gilded Cuff
The Gilded Cage
The Gilded Chain
Her British Stepbrother
Forbidden: Her British Stepbrother
Seduction: Her British Stepbrother
Climax: Her British Stepbrother

Paranormal
Dark Seductions Series
The Shadows of Stormclyffe Hall
The Love Bites Series
The Bite of Winter
Brotherhood of the Blood Moon Series
Blood Moon on the Rise (coming soon)
Brothers of Ash and Fire
Grigori: A Royal Dragon Romance
Mikhail: A Royal Dragon Romance (coming soon)
Rurik: A Royal Dragon Romance (coming soon)

Sci-Fi Romance
Cyborg Genesis Series
Across the Stars (coming soon)

Lauren
SMITH
TIMELESS ROMANCE

ABOUT THE AUTHOR

Lauren Smith is an Oklahoma attorney by day, author by night who pens adventurous and edgy romance stories by the light of her smart phone flashlight app. She knew she was destined to be a romance writer when she attempted to re-write the entire *Titanic* movie just to save Jack from drowning. Connecting with readers by writing emotionally moving, realistic and sexy romances no matter what time period is her passion. She's won multiple awards in several romance subgenres including: New England Reader's Choice Awards,

Greater Detroit BookSeller's Best Awards, and a Semi-Finalist award for the Mary Wollstonecraft Shelley Award.

To Connect with Lauren, visit her at:
www.laurensmithbooks.com
lauren@laurensmithbooks.com

CPSIA information can be obtained
at www.ICGtesting.com
Printed in the USA
LVHW110952291222
736137LV00009B/128

9 781947 206144